Secret seduction . . .

"Please don't run away," Louis pleaded. "I know you're upset. And I don't blame you. You want an explanation."

"No, I don't," Jessica shouted. "You're going to tell me that you don't owe me an explanation because there's nothing between us. I can't stand to hear you say it."

"Then I won't say it," he said, leaning over and kissing her with more passion and intensity than he had before.

In the privacy of the valley between the high dunes, Louis did his best to dispel, once and for all, any doubts Jessica might have had about his feelings for her.

Moments later, he put his fingers to her lips. "No one can know about us," he whispered. "No one, Jessica."

Bantam Books in the Sweet Valley University series:

SWEET VALLEY UNIVERSITY®

The Other Woman

Written by
Laurie John

Created by
FRANCINE PASCAL

BANTAM BOOKS
NEW YORK · TORONTO · LONDON · SYDNEY · AUCKLAND

THE OTHER WOMAN
A BANTAM BOOK : 0 553 50374 X

Originally published in U.S.A. by Bantam Books

First publication in Great Britain

PRINTING HISTORY
Bantam edition published 1996

The trademarks "Sweet Valley" and "Sweet Valley University"
are owned by Francine Pascal and are used under license by
Bantam Books and Transworld Publishers Ltd.

Conceived by Francine Pascal

Produced by Daniel Weiss Associates, Inc,
33 West 17th Street, New York, NY 10011

Bantam Books are published by Transworld Publishers Ltd,
61–63 Uxbridge Road, Ealing, London W5 5SA,
in Australia by Transworld Publishers (Australia) Pty Ltd,
15–25 Helles Avenue, Moorebank, NSW 2170,
and in New Zealand by Transworld Publishers (NZ) Ltd,
3 William Pickering Drive, Albany, Auckland.

Printed and bound in Great Britain by
Cox & Wyman Ltd, Reading, Berkshire.

To Sonja Carson Allen

Chapter One

"Jessica, stop," Louis Miles whispered hoarsely, brushing his lips against her ear. Her arms were wrapped around his neck and he reached up, gently disentangling himself. "I—I can't do this. This is wrong."

But even as he said it, his grasp on Jessica's arms weakened, and she felt his body surrender to his emotions. His large, graceful hands followed the line of her back, wrapped around the curve of her waist, and pulled her toward him in an even tighter embrace.

Jessica trembled as his lips traveled from her ear to her cheek and then down her neck before finding her mouth again. It was as if he were trying to memorize her face—the shape of her cheekbones, the texture of her skin, and the temperature of her lips.

Her heart pounding against his chest, Jessica began to shake. No kiss or embrace had ever made her feel as weak or as reckless. Not even ex-husband Mike McAllery's. Jessica's arms tightened again around his neck. This time Professor Miles didn't protest or try to pull away. She sank back, and they fell against the door of the car. The handle pressed into the small of Jessica's back, but she didn't care. She didn't care about anything.

"Oh, Jessica . . ." His breath was ragged as he pressed his lips against her hair.

Jessica parted her lips to say something, but his mouth covered hers before she could utter a word. The feel of his hands pressing against her shoulder blades drove away every thought but one—she was in love.

She was in love with Professor Louis Miles. He was young, handsome, and sexier than any man she had ever known.

The torrential rain beat heavily against the windshield, drawing a discreet gray curtain between them and anyone who might have passed the silver Toyota they were parked in . . . a few blocks from the Sweet Valley University campus.

After several minutes, Jessica became aware that the drumming sound on the windshield had begun to fade away. The rain was slacking off.

Professor Miles drew back, breathing as if he'd been running. He slowly released her.

Jessica's breath came in shallow gulps. In the aftermath of their passion, she could think of nothing to say, suddenly feeling overcome with shyness. Her foggy brain began to clear and her cheeks flushed with embarrassment.

She sat up and stared forward, straightening her skirt and sweater and surreptitiously wiping away the lipstick that she knew was smeared across her lips.

Professor Miles also seemed to be struggling to collect his thoughts and pull himself together. He sat up in his seat and took some deep breaths. "Jessica, I'm sorry," he whispered. He took her hand and gently pressed her fingertips against his own. "This can't happen again."

Jessica withdrew her hand and felt her shoulders hunch in almost unbearable humiliation. He was rejecting her. Her long blond hair hung down on either side of her face and she was glad for its protection.

His finger pushed back the curtain of hair in Jessica's eyes and gently tucked it behind her ear. "This isn't good for either one of us. It can't work."

"Why not?" Jessica asked quietly. She fought the tears that welled in the corners of her large, blue-green eyes. Her eyelashes were naturally thick and dark—which was fortunate. It had been an emotional roller coaster of a day, and even though Jessica's psyche felt battered and bruised, thankfully the afternoon's tears had left no black mascara marks on her smooth, golden cheeks.

Professor Miles sighed deeply, staring out the window. From the corner of her eye, Jessica could see the muscles of his strong jaw tense. "This is . . ." He rubbed his temples, as if he was searching for the just the right words. "This is inappropriate," he finally said.

"Inappropriate?" Jessica repeated miserably.

"You don't want to be with me because it's *inappropriate*. What does that mean? Are you embarrassed to be with me?"

"It means you're a wonderful girl and I'm trying to do what's right for you." He laughed wryly and with a touch of sorrow. "And yes, I *am* embarrassed. I've made a fool of myself over a beautiful student. What I've done is not fair. It's not ethical. I'm older than you are. I'm your *teacher*, Jessica. I've taken advantage of your youth and your trust, and I'm ashamed of myself. I'm not a suitable boyfriend for you. For all kinds of reasons."

He thinks I'm just a silly schoolgirl. A girl who knows nothing about love, Jessica thought. She lifted her chin and gathered up her courage. If she wanted Professor Miles to treat her like a woman, she had to act like a woman, not a naive teenager. "What reasons?" she asked in a more forceful voice, looking him straight in the eye.

"You wouldn't understand."

"Then explain it," she challenged. "Explain what you're doing to me. Tell me why you came looking for me after I left your office this afternoon. Tell me why you just kissed me like no one has ever kissed me before. Tell me why you're saying you made a fool out of yourself when I'm the one who feels like a total fool." Jessica's voice broke, and she was perilously close to tears again. "I can't believe you're pushing me away after we just . . ." She turned her face away, too embarrassed to verbalize what they had shared in the privacy of the rain.

4

"Jessica. I'm sorry. My feelings for you are . . ." His lips pressed together, and he shook his head. "I think it's pretty obvious what my feelings are," he said in a low tone. "Being a professor, I should be able to express myself in some florid and romantic way." He worked his shoulders, loosening the fit of his tweed jacket as if it was suddenly constricting him. He turned to face her. "But I'm afraid I've never felt more juvenile in my life. Or more filled with regret. As attracted to you as I am, and as intrigued and charmed and delighted and entranced and . . ." He trailed off, smiling wistfully. "This just can't go any further," he whispered.

"But why?" she cried. "Because I'm too young? Well, you're wrong," she protested. "I know you think I'm just a dizzy freshman girl. But I'm not." She gave him a crooked grin. "Okay. Well, maybe I *am* a dizzy freshman girl sometimes. But that doesn't have anything to do with my age. On some level, I'll probably be a dizzy freshman girl until the day I die."

Louis Miles laughed, making his emerald green eyes twinkle and his wavy brown hair tumble forward. He pushed it back, revealing the perfect widow's peak that gave his masculine face a sensitive beauty.

"But that doesn't mean I'm not an adult. I *am* an adult. I've even been married."

His eyebrows lifted in surprise.

"Don't look so shocked. It didn't last long. What I'm trying to tell you is that I've had relationships that were important. And I understand that things aren't always easy and . . . I wouldn't expect you to act like a *boyfriend*," she blurted, imitating the ironic tone he had used when he'd said the word. "I mean, I know it would be embarrassing for you to go to formals and all that stuff. I wouldn't expect you to. That would be . . . *inappropriate*." She dropped her voice, giving the word a deep and comically academic intonation.

He laughed again, leaning back against the seat. "You're so funny," he murmured. "And so sweet. In a saner world, I'd happily be your boyfriend. I'd take you to the homecoming formal or anywhere else you wanted to go. But in the real world, this relationship creates a lot of problems."

"Name one," she challenged.

Professor Miles leaned forward, turning the key in the ignition. "My job."

"Okay, name two."

"My job."

"Name three."

He laughed again but didn't answer this time. He pulled out into the wet street, and they drove in silence for two blocks until they reached a stoplight. Students darted back and forth across the street. Some carried the large SVU umbrellas that were sold at the campus bookstore. Others huddled under sheets of newspaper, using them as protection from the drizzling rain.

"Which dorm are you in?" Professor Miles

asked when the light changed and the car was in motion again.

"Dickenson," Jessica answered, looking at him.

He acknowledged her answer with a nod, and they circled the perimeter of the campus, taking the long way to the entrance behind Dickenson Hall.

Jessica turned and stared out the window, her emotions in a jumble. Ever since she'd met Professor Miles in the bookstore at the beginning of the semester, there had been something special between them. Something more than a friendship. She'd been able to laugh and joke with him in a way she never had with a teacher before, and he'd become essential to her happiness.

Now she was sitting in his silver Toyota, trying to deal with the fact that he'd just told her they should cool things off . . . before they had even begun. Jessica closed her eyes, her heart pounding at the memory of that first kiss just a few minutes ago. No one had ever kissed her as passionately. No one had ever held her as possessively. And she had never returned any man's kiss as eagerly as she'd returned his.

"Jessica." His gentle voice prompted her to open her eyes. When she looked out the window, she saw that they had arrived at the back entrance of her dormitory. Professor Miles pulled up in front of the rear door. He didn't turn off the engine, and Jessica knew he was waiting for her to get out.

But she didn't want to leave. She wanted to be with him. Wherever he was going from here, she wanted to go to—whether it was home, the movies, the dry cleaners, or the gas station. "I want to stay with you," she said bluntly.

He shook his head. "No," he said quietly. "It's just too dangerous."

"Because of your job?"

He paused and then nodded. "That's right. Because of my job."

But there was something unconvincing about the nod. She smiled. "You don't seem like a man who'd be afraid to risk his job for true love."

"You don't know me very well," he said kindly. He leaned across her lap, opened the door, and pushed it wider for her. "You'd better go in. You're soaking wet, and it's cold out there."

Jessica reluctantly climbed out of the car, then leaned down to take a last look at his beautiful face—his high, masculine brow, firm jaw, and full mouth.

Jessica knew how much his work meant to him. And she knew that teaching jobs were hard to come by. Her rational mind knew Louis Miles was right. He'd wanted to teach his whole life. And since he was a new professor at SVU, a relationship with a student would almost certainly cost him his job.

"Good-bye . . . Professor Miles," she whispered, a lump rising in her throat. She closed the door, turning quickly before he could see the tears.

Jessica put her hands against the heavy glass door that led to the back lobby and pushed. As the door swung open, she heard him shout.

"Jessica! Jessica, wait!"

She paused and then turned. Louis Miles was outside the car on the driver's side, the gentle rain falling down the collar of his jacket.

"Louis," he said.

"What?" she choked out.

"Call me Louis." He lifted his hand, giving her a faint wave before he climbed back inside the car and drove away.

Jessica waved back, watching the car until the last glimmer of taillight had disappeared into the fog.

"Five-nothing," Elizabeth called out, settling herself more comfortably on the hood of Todd's car while she kept score.

Daryl Cartright dribbled the basketball right past Todd, took a running jump, and slam-dunked the ball. The basketball hoop that was mounted over the garage door of Daryl's shabby one-story ranch was bent in several places. And it wasn't hard to see why.

The ball hit the rim of the net with so much impact, it made a reverberating sound that echoed against the cracked concrete driveway.

"Yes!" Daryl said, lifting his right arm up, fist closed, in happiness.

"Six-nothing," Elizabeth said, holding up five fingers on her right hand and one on her left.

"The game's not over yet, man," Todd Wilkins said, abandoning his laid-back guard tactics and aggressively attacking the ball.

Daryl never missed a beat as he caught the ball on the rebound and dribbled it, keeping his back to Todd as he moved left and right.

Daryl took several steps to the right and then, in an abrupt move, he pulled left and skirted Todd with a fake. He roared toward the hoop and sent the ball sailing through the air with such precision that it made no noise at all when it fell through the net without touching the rim.

Todd threw up his hands in surrender when the ball hit the driveway with a loud smack. He wiped the sweat running off his brow and laughed. "I give up. And besides, I'm not dressed for a serious game. These jeans and shirt aren't helping my moves on the court."

Daryl grinned and grabbed the ball. He spun it on his fingertip and dribbled it a couple of times back and forth under his legs before tossing the ball into the pile of rickety bicycles and spare auto parts littering the far end of the drive. "Don't blame the jeans," he teased. "You're out of practice and out of shape."

Daryl wiped his forehead with the shoulder of the green T-shirt he wore with baggy black shorts. Elizabeth couldn't help feeling the gesture was reflexive. Daryl Cartright had just put Todd Wilkins through a half an hour of hard one-on-one, and he hadn't even broken a sweat.

Panting, Todd put his hands on his hips. "You're right. I am out of practice. You're in great shape, though. So how do you explain your slump last year?"

The smile abruptly left Daryl Cartright's face, and he ran a hand over his short red hair. "Yeah. Well, listen, Wilkins, it's always nice to see another basketball player and throw a few hoops, but I gotta go on inside. Thanks for coming by." He turned on his heel and walked toward the door of the house.

Elizabeth jumped off the hood of Todd's car. "Todd was a star SVU forward, Daryl, and I just watched you play rings around him. Eight colleges wanted you last year. You picked SVU. After three games, your game fell apart. After five games, you were gone. What happened?"

Daryl said nothing and didn't turn around. "Was it drugs?" Todd shouted. "Did you start using drugs? Is that why your game fell off?"

Daryl skidded to a stop and whipped around to face them. His face was so angry that Elizabeth had to fight the impulse to hang on to Todd's sleeve for protection.

"You listen to me, man. And you listen good. I have *never* touched drugs in my life. Anybody who *thinks* I did is wrong. Anybody who *says* I did is a liar." Daryl turned back toward the house, walking with an angry, determined step. The muscles in his long, powerful legs flexed with every step. They were the legs of an athlete. A first-class athlete.

"I don't think you messed with any drugs," Elizabeth called out as Daryl put his hand on the doorknob and yanked open the screen door. "I don't think you were a flash in the pan, either. You want to know what I *do* think?" she challenged.

11

He turned again and directed a fierce glare in her direction, as if daring her to say anything else. "No," he yelled. "I don't care what you think."

"I'll tell you what I think anyway," Elizabeth shouted, refusing to back down.

"Well, then come tell me in the house," Daryl roared at the top of his voice like a man goaded beyond endurance. "You don't have to tell the neighbors everything that's on your mind." The screen door slammed shut behind him with a loud bang.

"I think we've been invited in," Elizabeth said to Todd.

"Come on," Todd said, gently taking her arm. "But watch your step, okay? You're coming on too strong. We need to know what he knows. We don't want to scare him off."

Elizabeth nodded, and they followed Daryl warily into the shabby house.

Once inside, Elizabeth looked around in surprise. The neighborhood outside Daryl's house was dilapidated, dispirited, and dotted with empty bottles and cans. But inside, his house was spotless.

There was a cheerful, domestic quality about the place. The furniture was cheap and worn out, but it was clean and polished. A patched red-and-white tablecloth covered the kitchen table, and bright childish drawings were taped to the door of the refrigerator. A juice bottle on the counter held a carefully arranged bouquet of lacy weeds and wildflowers plucked from the overgrown yards of the neighboring houses.

Somebody in this household cared.

"Where are your folks?" Todd asked, looking around the room.

"Don't have any," Daryl said shortly.

Elizabeth and Todd exchanged a look and Todd shrugged, obviously mystified.

"A wife?" Elizabeth ventured.

Daryl didn't answer. He sat down at the kitchen table, leaned on his elbows, and pushed back the other two chairs with his foot. "Sit," he said curtly.

Elizabeth and Todd took their seats.

"Now," Daryl began, "let's quit playing games. Why are you two here? What do you want?"

Elizabeth crossed her arms over her chest. "We're looking for some answers to a big puzzle. You were a star player last year. A sure thing for the pros. Then suddenly, your game fell apart. You blew baskets. You dropped the ball. You got fouled. You lost your temper on the court and got benched. You didn't live up to your high school reputation."

Daryl shrugged. "It happens. Not everybody in the college game is pro material. I wasn't." He leaned back in his chair, balancing on the back two legs.

"Did somebody pay you to drop the ball?" Elizabeth asked bluntly.

Daryl fell forward, and the legs of his chair made a loud thump on the floor. "What are you talking about?" he asked evenly.

"I'm talking about point shaving," Elizabeth

answered. "Holding down the score. Controlling the point spread. Fixing games."

"For who?"

"You tell me," Elizabeth said.

"I'm telling you to leave."

Cheat.

It was an ugly word.

Winston sat at his desk and stared at his notebook. Hidden inside the front flap was a copy of tomorrow's physics test.

A *stolen* copy.

Winston Egbert—formerly a young man of sterling character, whose only sin was a fondness for bad puns and practical jokes—had stolen a copy of the exam.

Winston was an incurable class clown. Nonetheless, his grades had always been excellent and a source of much pride to his father and mother.

Physics 101, however, had been Winston's Waterloo.

He had spent no time at all studying the subject and now he had a major exam on the horizon. He was way underprepared.

Winston had begged his physics teacher, Professor Stark, for some extra-credit work to bring up his grade. Professor Stark had originally refused, but after much begging, pleading, and wheedling on Winston's part, he'd agreed to prepare some study guides for Winston that might help him pass the next test.

Professor Stark hadn't been in the office he temporarily shared with Professor Miles- when Winston had arrived to pick up the study guides earlier that afternoon. But Jessica Wakefield had been. She was waiting there for Professor Miles, and she had let Winston into the office.

Winston had glanced over Professor Stark's cluttered desk for an envelope with his name on it. But right there, on top of the desk, he'd seen something much more interesting—the stack of xeroxed exams only partially covered by a textbook.

A million thoughts had flashed through Winston's head. His physics grade was pathetic. According to his calculations, unless he aced the test tomorrow, he'd probably receive a failing grade for the semester. The *best*-case scenario was a D.

Winston Egbert knew his father well enough to know that a D, or for that matter a C, was not acceptable. A's were what his parents expected from the scion of the Egbert household, and A's they usually got. The occasional B slid by with a wink and a chuckling admonition to "buckle down."

Winston grabbed two big handfuls of his curly chestnut hair and pulled. If he made an F, his parents were going to be upset. Very upset.

They would yell. They would scream. They would make many phone calls. They would call Grandma Egbert, the matriarch. She would call Uncle Fred, the analyst. They would call Aunt May, the experimental education proponent.

They'd blame the television. They'd blame the

15

school. And then they'd blame themselves. "Where did we go wrong?" his mother would wail. "Did we push too hard?"

Then, when the hysteria level dropped and the dust settled, they'd start looking for an explanation—something a little more concrete than overdoses of mass popular culture and too much pressure during Winston's Little League years.

Finally, they'd arrive at the truth. And they weren't going to like it.

Denise Waters . . . the love of his life.

"Oh, Denise. I've gotten myself into a doozy this time," Winston said to himself, picturing his beautiful, intelligent girlfriend.

Winston was addicted to her company. And Denise seemed to be pretty crazy about him, too. Together they played, socialized, ordered strange concoctions of pizza, watched old movies into the wee hours, and procrastinated on their schoolwork.

But there was one major difference. Denise could procrastinate with the best of them, but when that old clock struck the eleventh hour, she energized and got her act together. The fact that she was brilliant, hardly had to study, and had an almost photographic memory didn't hurt. Her grades were pretty solid—all A's.

Winston's academic record was feeling the strain of having too much fun. If his parents thought he couldn't handle the distractions of college, they just might decide he wasn't mature enough to be at SVU. They might try to move him to a smaller, more academically oriented school.

Leaving SVU meant leaving Denise. The thought of being separated from Denise gave him a pain in his heart that was so intense it practically knocked him to the floor.

He had only one choice. Cheat!

Winston hadn't worked up the courage to look at the stolen test yet. But it was now or never. With a shaking hand, he opened the notebook and gingerly removed the exam.

Very quietly, as if he were afraid someone might pop out of the closet and catch him red-handed, he unfolded the paper.

He stared at it, puzzling. There were lots of problem sets, but he'd done enough reading to know where to find the answers in his textbook. It would take a while, but if he stayed up most of the night, he could commit them to memory and ace the test tomorrow.

Cheat!

Looking at the test in advance was cheating, and cheating was wrong.

But I'm doing it for Denise. . . . Which meant that he was doing it for love. Could anything really be wrong if you were doing it for love?

Chapter Two

"Liz, are you home?" Jessica called out as she opened the door of the room she shared with her twin sister, Elizabeth. "Oh, well, guess not."

Both girls had the same shoulder-length blond hair, the same blue-green eyes, and the same dimples in their left cheeks. But when it came to personalities, Jessica and Elizabeth Wakefield were polar opposites.

Jessica looked around their room. As usual, her studious sibling's half of the room was neat, well organized, and indicated a serious interest in academics and broadcast journalism. Books about famous newscasters like Walter Cronkite were stacked on top of reference materials and news magazines. Next to Elizabeth's computer were several videocassettes ready to be returned to WSVU, the campus television station. Elizabeth worked there with her boyfriend, Tom Watts, the handsome news anchor and general manager.

Jessica's side of the room, on the other hand, revealed a very different personality—a personality that was impulsive, reckless, impatient, and passionate. "Louis was right," Jessica said, moving over to her side of the room. "This is the room of an immature teenage girl," she said unhappily to no one in particular.

Jessica had always been interested in parties, men, her sorority, and fun—not necessarily in that order. Trashy romances were stacked beside her bed. Clothes were strewn across every surface. And her bureau was littered with cosmetics, invitations, and telephone messages taken by an accommodating Elizabeth.

Jessica picked up one of the romances and grimaced. Suddenly the couple on the book jacket looked totally ridiculous. A handsome male with long, flowing hair held a woman whose chest bulged out of a low-cut, eighteenth-century dress.

How could Jessica have ever been moved by something so phony and unreal? The emotions depicted in the book were as superficial and silly as the illustration on the cover.

The book made a thunking sound when Jessica dropped it into the metal wastebasket. There was no point in keeping it. She knew she'd never take any pleasure in stories of make-believe love again.

Now that I've found my true love . . . Professor Louis Miles.

How incredibly ironic. After her short marriage

to Mike McAllery, her destructive encounter with James Montgomery, and her ultimately disappointing relationship with Randy Mason, Jessica had sworn off men forever. Love was too painful, filled with turmoil and disappointment. She'd been hurt too many times to take another risk.

Mike, her ex-husband, had been exciting but dangerous. He'd drawn them both into an escalating circle of emotional violence that had finally culminated in a tragic accident involving a gun.

James Montgomery had tried to rape her. She could hardly bear thinking about *that*.

And Randy Mason? *Ha!* Jessica had to laugh. Randy had been sweet and protective to a degree, but ultimately he too had fallen short of her ideal. Or more accurately, she had fallen short of his.

And now there was Louis Miles.

Jessica walked over to her desk and sat down, running her fingers over her Medieval History text. Professor Miles—*Louis,* she mentally corrected herself—had inspired her with a real desire to excel in his subject.

She had worked hard on her essay on Tristan and Isolde, that pair of tragic lovers. And in the process, just as Louis had predicted, Jessica had found her lost sense of romantic wonder.

Smiling, she pulled the creased, rain-spattered essay from her purse. Jessica lifted the paper to her lips, then crumpled it against her breast. Louis was right. There were problems with the two of them dating. He didn't see any solutions. And right now, neither did she. If his job was important to him, then it was important to her. Nothing mattered more than Louis's happiness.

No matter how hard Louis pushed her away, Jessica knew he cared about her. And when people truly cared about each other, somehow, somewhere, they found a way to be together. Now she just had to come up with a foolproof plan. . . .

"Listen, Daryl," Todd said softly, trying to calm Daryl down. "We're not out to get you in trouble. We're just trying to figure out what's going on. Liz and I believe a gambling syndicate is controlling the Sweet Valley University athletics department."

"You don't know what you're talking about, man. What made you think such a crazy thing?" Daryl demanded.

"Well, how about big sums of money donated to the athletics budget by anonymous alumni? The records say the money was used for new lockers and gym flooring. But I've never seen any new lockers, and I can tell you the gym still needs reflooring. So where did the money go?"

Daryl shrugged. "Recruiting, probably. They slipped some players money under the table to play for SVU. It happens. It happens a lot." He glanced at Todd. "*You* should know that. You got kicked off the team because of a recruiting scandal. You and Mark Gathers." He cocked his head and stared quizzically at Elizabeth. "And weren't you the reporter who broke the story?"

"Yeah," Todd admitted. "But that scandal wasn't about money. It was about special privileges—things like reserved parking spaces and better dorm rooms. I never got offered any money during recruiting. And neither did Mark Gathers."

"They kicked you off the team because of a parking spot?" Daryl said in a voice of mild surprise. "That doesn't seem like much of a scandal."

"Actually, I was *suspended*. Now I'm trying to get reinstated."

"So what's the problem? How am I involved?"

Todd drummed his fingers on the kitchen table. "According to Dr. Beal, the head of administration, the Alumni Association is extremely concerned about the reputation of the athletics department. They don't want even a whiff of scandal associated with them or any of the teams. It tends to *'negatively impact alumni donations.'*"

Daryl snorted, as if he were amused by something incredibly ironic.

Elizabeth raised her eyebrows and looked at Todd. He sat slightly forward, tense and alert. "So you *do* know something . . ." Todd pressed.

Daryl stared across the table at Todd with a stony expression, clearly determined to say nothing.

Elizabeth jumped in. "We put two and two together and came up with what we think is the real explanation. We think somebody is paying players to shave points and then disappear before anybody can catch on."

Daryl shook his head again as if he couldn't

22

quite believe how naive they were. "Let me get this straight. You got kicked off the team over a parking spot, and now you want me to say I took money to fix games for gamblers, which, by the way, is illegal. *And you're not here to get me into any trouble.*" He laughed, but there was no mirth in his voice. "I'd like to know what your definition of *trouble* is." He laughed again and then cocked an questioning eyebrow. "You know, you never answered my question before. Why did you come to *me*?"

"Because you were the most obvious example. Once we came up with the theory, your name sprang immediately to mind. You had a great game, it went sour, and then you were gone. We thought maybe if we came out and talked to you, you might give us some information that could help."

Daryl stood, went over to the sink, and turned on the faucet. He sprayed water over his face, then grabbed a towel, vigorously rubbing himself dry. He was obviously agitated. And now, Elizabeth noticed, he really was sweating. "I think you guys better leave," he said. Daryl seemed to be holding in his temper.

"How much did you get?" Todd pressed.

Daryl opened a pantry door and took out a box of spaghetti and a couple of cans of tomato paste. "Listen, I'm busy. I don't have time for your crazy theories. It's time for you to go."

Todd stood and threw out his hands in frustration. "C'mon, Daryl," he cried, his voice full of genuine sorrow. "You had everything going for you. How could they possible pay you enough to throw away a career in the pros?"

Daryl banged the cans down on the counter and looked as if he were going to explode. "You listen to me—" he began, pointing an angry finger at Todd.

The kitchen door opened, and Daryl broke off immediately. Elizabeth and Todd turned and saw a little girl around eight years old peering in the doorway with a frightened look on her face. "What's wrong?" she asked Daryl in a shy, little girl voice.

Daryl's entire body changed. His face softened and his glower disappeared. "Nothing's wrong, sweetie. Come on over here and help me fix dinner."

The door opened with some difficulty, and the girl entered. Her little head had two long, dark braids, each of them tied with a bright blue ribbon that matched her freshly pressed blue jumper. On each leg she wore heavy metal braces attached to corrective shoes, and she walked with the help of crutches.

She smiled at Todd and Elizabeth, and they smiled back. "Hi," Elizabeth said. "I'm Liz, and this is Todd. We're friends of Daryl's from school." She shot an inquisitive look at Daryl.

Daryl sat down on a chair and pulled the little girl onto his lap. "This is Lucy," he said in a voice full of pride. "My little sister."

Lucy pointed to the large, colorful crayon drawing on the refrigerator door. "I did that. It was the best one in my class."

Todd walked over and examined it very solemnly. "I don't know much about art, but I know what I like. And I like that picture very much."

Lucy climbed down from Daryl's lap, removed the picture, and put it in Todd's hands. "Here," she said shyly. "You can keep it."

"Thank you," Todd replied with a pleased look. "I'll put it in my room and think of you when I look at it."

"No," she said quietly. "Think of Daryl. He doesn't ever have friends come over. Will you come over again sometime?"

Elizabeth shot a look at Daryl, who was obviously embarrassed by his little sister's revelations. "Are your brothers home?" Daryl asked, changing the subject.

"James is home. Pike is over at Peter's."

Daryl's face darkened with displeasure. "Tell James to go over to Peter's and bring Pike home, please. Dinner's in half an hour."

Lucy cast a knowing look at Elizabeth and Todd. "Daryl doesn't like Peter," she confided. "Peter's in a gang."

"Go on," Daryl urged in a stern tone.

She lifted her head haughtily, making it clear she was unimpressed with his authoritarian act. She lifted her fingers and waved at Todd and Elizabeth. "Bye," she whispered.

"Bye," Elizabeth and Todd echoed.

When she was gone, there was a long silence.

"She's adorable," Elizabeth commented.

Daryl fidgeted with the package of spaghetti. "Those kids are all the family I got," he said quietly. "My daddy died when I was a kid. Mom died two years back. I'm the oldest. I gotta look out for them. It's a full-time job. It didn't leave a lot of time for basketball practice. It affected my game."

"I don't believe that," Todd said.

Daryl looked at Todd, and his eyes narrowed. "I don't care what you believe."

"Maybe nobody paid you anything," Todd said thoughtfully, his eyes studying Daryl's face. "Maybe somebody threatened you. Or threatened somebody close to you."

Elizabeth's mouth fell open. That hadn't occurred to her. She put a concerned hand on Daryl's arm. "Is that so? Did somebody threaten you? Did they threaten to do anything to your sister and brothers?"

"Nobody threatened me," Daryl said, shaking off Elizabeth's hand. "Nobody forced me to do anything I didn't want to do." Daryl's jaw muscles tensed, and Elizabeth held her breath.

Elizabeth closed her eyes unhappily. She realized they weren't going to get any cooperation from Daryl Cartright, and she couldn't blame him. She'd probably do the same thing herself. Todd carefully rolled up the picture Lucy had given him and put it under his arm. Elizabeth followed him out of the kitchen and into the drive.

Daryl stood in the doorway, watching them.

Todd snapped his fingers, as if he had just remembered something, and turned. "Daryl, there's something I didn't tell you."

"Oh, yeah?"

"Yeah." Todd's voice was conversational and genial. "A couple of nights ago, two guys mugged me in the parking lot on campus. They said to warn my girlfriend to stop asking so many questions."

Daryl's face remained impassive. "If you talk to them," Todd said, "tell them Elizabeth's not my girlfriend, will you?"

"I don't plan on talking to anybody about anything," Daryl responded in a flat voice.

"You're not a bad guy, Cartright," Todd said. "Neither am I. And neither is Liz. Campus information has our numbers if you decide you want to talk to us."

"I won't," Daryl said. "And Wilkins . . ."

"Yeah?"

"Don't come back here. I've got nothing to say to you." Daryl shut the door with a slam.

Louis stood in front of the double-glass doors of his beachfront condo and looked out into the night. The afternoon storm had returned, and over the last hour the weather had become increasingly violent.

Thunder crashed and great jagged streaks of lightning illuminated the ocean. Turbulent black waves curled eight and ten feet into the air before crashing down, creating an eerie white foam.

27

Louis hated this kind of weather. It was too volatile. Too emotional and out of control. It disturbed him and made him think of . . .

He pushed away the thought and walked into the dark kitchen just in time to hear the whistle of the teakettle. Without turning on the lights, he located the tin of loose tea that sat on the shelf over the oven.

Still in the dark Louis made his tea, sweetened it with honey, and located a spoon. He'd gotten used to moving through the unlit condo, and he felt safer with all the lights off. It created the impression that no one was at home.

Unfortunately, he couldn't work without a lamp.

Who am I kidding? I'm not going to get any work done tonight. Not with thoughts of Jessica so fresh in his memory. He could still hear the sound of her laugh echoing in his mind, and his fingertips tingled with the phantom feel of her silky hair. He sipped his tea, and the sweet taste reminded him of her lips.

Louis closed his eyes, groaning out loud. "Oh, Jessica. If only things could be different. If only I could explain."

Suddenly his heart slowed, and the hair on the back of his neck stood up. He sniffed the air. Was there a trace of rose perfume in the air? It was a scent he recognized instantly . . . a scent he dreaded.

When Louis put down his tea mug, his hand nudged the edge of a votive candle jar. He

28

breathed a sigh of relief. No. There was no rose perfume in the air. He was smelling the remnants of the scented candles he had burned when he'd moved in. They had erased the musty, empty-house smell that had lingered after the departure of the last tenants.

The condo was nice, though not as luxurious as the ones farther down the beach. All in all, Louis was happy with it. It was decorated in soft beach hues. The cotton-covered sofa and chairs were putty and pale green. The walls were a soothing taupe. Muted watercolors hung over the fireplace. There were very few ornaments and very little color. He liked the condo because it was the only thing in his life that was simple. In the dark, it was even simpler.

Louis took another sip of his tea and tried to relax. He hadn't turned on a light since he'd returned from campus.

She won't come here tonight. Not if she thinks no one's home.

Shrugging on a slicker, Louis stepped outside onto the deck. The overhang from the house protected him from the worst of the rain, and he sat on a wooden chair, both his hands around the mug to keep them warm.

His heart was heavy and sad, but at the same time, he was elated. It felt good to be in love, even if it was a forbidden love.

He'd had his barriers up for so long, he'd forgotten what it was like to touch and be touched.

29

It seemed like a million years since he'd cared and had someone to care for him in return.

Love was impossible. It was an exercise in heartbreak. And it was too dangerous. He'd resigned himself to a loveless existence a long time ago, and he'd made up his mind to accept the limitations of his life without complaint.

He hadn't counted on meeting Jessica Wakefield, though. She was the first woman to break through the emotional barriers he had erected around himself. And she had pierced the vulnerable and tender part of his heart like a laser beam. The feelings she produced were almost unbearably painful and at the same time, unbearably pleasurable.

But there could be nothing between them. Nothing. For her own good, Louis needed to turn away from her. Never see her or speak with her privately.

He looked out into the tumultuous night and something like hatred blazed in his heart, momentarily obliterating every other emotion.

The mug in his hands shattered and he looked down, startled. His hands were balled into fists. Tiny shards of pottery clung to his palms, each one drawing a small drop of his blood.

Elizabeth sighed. "I don't know about you, but I'm more convinced than ever that we're on the right track."

"Me too," Todd said. "We just need some facts. Something besides hunches and theories and angry ex-basketball players telling us to get our big noses out of their business."

Todd and Elizabeth walked across the wet campus. They'd driven back to SVU through a horrible downpour. It was over now, and all that was left of the violent weather was a light fog hovering over a bunch of puddles.

A truck was parked on the curb with its tail blocking the walkway. No workmen were in sight, and a pile of soggy lumber and rusty pipe was strewn across the broken sidewalk. Todd took Elizabeth's arm, steering her around it. "That truck's been there for two weeks," he commented irritably. "And I haven't seen one workman. In fact, there are half-finished building projects all over the campus and no workmen anywhere."

"Maybe it's because of the weather. There's been a lot of rain lately," Elizabeth answered absently. Her mind was clearly still on Daryl and their investigation of the point-shaving scheme. "Let's figure out what we've got and where our investigation will lead us next," she said, her tone turning brisk and businesslike. She paused outside the student union building. "Let's get something to eat while we do this," she said. "I'm starving."

"Me too," Todd said, suddenly aware of a gnawing feeling in his stomach. The SVU Snack Caf was located in the basement. "I was hoping Daryl would invite us to stay for some of that pasta," he said as he followed her inside the student union.

"I don't think we should count on any dinner invitations from Daryl. *Don't come back* pretty much means he's not interested in cultivating our friendship."

"You've got a point," Todd said grimly as they walked through the empty entrance hall and descended the steps that led to the basement. At the bottom of the stairs, a large sign announced that the Snack Caf was temporarily closed for repairs. "Still!" Elizabeth sighed impatiently. "They started those repairs three weeks ago." She looked at her watch. "And the cafeteria's probably closed by now."

"Want to drive into town and get a pizza?" Todd asked.

She shook her head. "Nah. I'm too tired. Let's see what's in the lounge."

They crossed the hall and entered the brightly lit room filled with long study tables and lots of snack machines. A few people sat at tables with their books and papers spread out before them. It wasn't a very attractive room, with its speckled linoleum, orange plastic chairs, and fluorescent lighting. But it was a good enough place to study, hang out, and eat junk food when there was nowhere else to go.

Todd dug down into his pockets and produced a handful of change. "Dinner's on me," he said with a laugh, holding up a few quarters. "Price is no object."

Elizabeth grinned and took some change from his palm. She began feeding it into the machine and punching buttons until they had an armload of potato chips, cheese popcorn, oatmeal cookies, and sodas. "Let's sit over there," Elizabeth said, nodding toward a private table in the corner. "I'll make the case—starting from the beginning. You play devil's advocate."

They took their seats, and Elizabeth began arranging the junk food on the table. "Okay," she said, biting down on a potato chip with an efficient crunch. "We need to figure out where all that money went." Elizabeth's fingers hovered over the table as she deliberated over her next bite of junk food. "The first logical assumption would be that they used it to recruit players. Just like Daryl said."

"But it's illegal for colleges to pay players." Todd opened a soda with a loud pop. "And we don't have any evidence of that happening here at SVU. When you confronted Coach Crane, he denied it. And then when you called a few players and asked them if they were ever offered money, they all said no. We don't have any way of knowing whether or not they're telling the truth, but I know for certain that *I* was never offered any money to play for SVU. All I got was a stupid parking spot." He glowered at Elizabeth. "An offense for which my good friend, Elizabeth Wakefield, spattered my name all over the news and got me kicked off the team."

Elizabeth put down her food and narrowed her eyes. "It was more than that and you know it. You guys got all kinds of special privileges, and it wasn't fair."

Todd held up his hands in a gesture of surrender. "Okay, okay. We did get preferential treatment. But it still wasn't illegal. So why is the administration so inflexible about reinstating me?"

Elizabeth leaned back in her chair and bit her lip. "That's what we're here to figure out."

Todd noticed people from other tables looking in their direction. He gave her a warning look. "We'd better keep our voices down. We don't want the entire student body to know about our investigation. At least not yet."

"Okay," Elizabeth said softly. "So if the money didn't go for recruiting, the next theory is that it went to pay players to fix games. Meaning they had to find guys who were good, but who were willing to take a dive. Guys like Daryl Cartright."

"Why would a player agree to it, though? Risk a career in the pros where they stand to make millions of bucks?" Todd asked.

"Maybe they couldn't wait that long to earn all that money in the pros. Maybe their parents died and they needed new braces for their sister's legs . . ." Elizabeth chewed moodily on a pretzel stick.

"Oh, man, this is so frustrating. So where do we go from here, Ms. Investigative Reporter?" Todd asked.

"We need to make a list," she said, seeming to rejuvenate with each bite of the pretzel. "A list of all the players like Daryl, who looked good at the beginning of the season, fell down on the job, and then disappeared." She reached for an oatmeal cookie.

Todd took a swig of his soda. "Are you sure you want to do this, Liz? If we're right and it turns out we can prove it, things could get dangerous."

Elizabeth nodded and threw him a dark look. "I know. But I can take care of myself."

He reached out and took the oatmeal cookie from her hand. "Seriously, Elizabeth, maybe we should both back off this. Maybe wait until Tom gets back from Las Vegas. I don't want you taking any chances because of me."

Elizabeth snatched the cookie back and nibbled irritably at the edge. "Tom Watts is an ex-football star, the head of the campus station, and my boyfriend. But he's not Superman, and we're not Lois Lane and Jimmy Olsen. We don't need Tom lurking in the background of every story to protect us."

"Speak for yourself. I wouldn't mind having Tom lurking in the background to protect me," Todd responded with a laugh. "I could have used him in the parking lot the other night."

"No way. I'm not waiting for Tom to get back from Las Vegas."

Todd lowered his head so she wouldn't see his amused smile. Elizabeth and Tom Watts were madly in love, but their relationship definitely had its ups and downs.

Tom, along with major figures from college stations all over the country, had been invited to Las Vegas as a guest of a new all-NCAA sports network that was about to premiere on cable. The student reporters would meet the network executives and attend workshops on sports broadcasting arranged for their benefit. The students at SVU were buzzing with excitement over the premiere event because it featured a wrestling match with their own star wrestler, Craig Maser, against a University of Arizona wrestler named Scotty Fisher.

Todd reached out and took Elizabeth's hand. "Listen, Liz. I'm not implying that you can't take care of yourself without Tom. But we need to be careful. These are not nice people we're dealing with."

"Which is exactly why I'm staying on this investigation." Elizabeth withdrew her hand, picked up a piece of cheese-flavored popcorn, and threw it at Todd.

Todd brushed the popcorn from his shirt. "Okay. I've done my duty as a colleague, ex-boyfriend, and surrogate brother. If you're in, you're in. And so am I. So let's make a list. Who do we talk to next?"

Elizabeth leaned forward on her elbows. "You know, this would be a lot easier with Gin-Yung on board."

Todd put down his pencil and pad, laced his fingers together on the table in front of him, and smiled to cover his growing sense of alarm. He'd wondered how long it was going to take Elizabeth to get to Gin-Yung.

Gin-Yung was Todd's girlfriend. She was a feisty Korean-American sportswriter with an encyclopedic knowledge of sports: statistics, history, lore, and gossip. Gin-Yung was the first girl Todd had been in love with since he'd broken up with Elizabeth at the beginning of their freshman year.

Not only didn't he want to risk getting Gin-Yung hurt, he didn't want to foul up his relationship with her by making her part of a threesome with Elizabeth.

Besides, he knew Elizabeth. He knew Gin-Yung. And he knew his own limitations. If the two of them ever joined forces, they'd roll right over him. He wouldn't have a chance. He'd lose control of this investigation completely. "No way," he said shortly. He unlaced his fingers, picked up his pencil, and began to make a note.

Elizabeth reached over and took his pencil. "Gin-Yung knows more about who's who in the sports world than you or I do. We need her."

"I don't want her involved."

"I promise not to do anything that would put her in any danger." She lifted her fingers with her thumb and little finger folded down. "Scout's honor."

Todd laughed, and Elizabeth handed him back one of his quarters.

"Call her. Tell her to meet us at the coffeehouse."

"Got any more quarters?" Elizabeth asked three hours later. "I want to play a song on the jukebox."

The coffeehouse was full. Groups of students sat at every table, talking over cups of exotic coffee and plates of cheesecake. The coffeehouse was the place to hang out if you wanted to talk books, politics, or art. The campus writers and intellectuals hung out there. It wasn't really Todd's scene. But Gin-Yung liked it and so did Elizabeth.

"What am I? Fort Knox?" Todd reached into his pocket, sorted through the remaining change, and dropped his last two quarters into Elizabeth's palm. "Here. That's it. You've cleaned me out."

"Play G-4," Gin-Yung instructed, taking a sip of her coffee. She smiled at Todd. "It's our song."

"G-4, it is," Elizabeth said pleasantly. "Any other requests?"

"Whatever you like," Todd answered, taking a bite of his cheesecake.

"Then I'll play T-2." Elizabeth chuckled. She patted Todd on the shoulder and winked at Gin-Yung. "That was our song."

Todd laughed, and Gin-Yung gave him a quizzical smile as Elizabeth walked toward the jukebox.

"It's nice that you two can still be such good friends," Gin-Yung said. There was a faint but unmistakable note of unease in her voice.

Todd immediately put down his . fork and reached across the table for her hand. "Not still," he corrected. "Again. Elizabeth and I went through a really rough time after we broke up. It wasn't easy to put our friendship back together. But that's all it is. A friendship. Don't get jealous."

Gin-Yung's delicate brows rose in indignation. "Jealous? You think I, Gin-Yung Suh, five-foot, one-inch star sportswriter for the *Sweet Valley Gazette,* could be threatened by a tall, willowy blonde you've known since the sixth grade?" She twitched the lapels of her navy blue blazer and shook the cuffs of her white shirt in a comical imitation of someone taking offense.

"Second," Todd corrected with an amused smile.

"Second grade," she amended. "Do you really think I'm the kind of girl who'd feel threatened in a situation like that?"

"Yes."

"And you're right," she said, pointing her index finger at him. "What's going on between you two? You've been together practically every day since this whole investigation started. Both of you pump me for information and then you don't tell me anything. I feel used and left out. Do you blame me for feeling jealous?"

Todd scrooched his chair closer to hers so they now sat side by side and could speak in lower tones. He saw a classmate approach Elizabeth and begin a conversation. "Okay. I'll bring you up to date. But only if you promise to stay out of it."

The humorous expression left her face. "Why? What's going on?"

"Things could get ugly from here on in, and I don't want you to get hurt."

"Who would hurt me?"

Todd rubbed the back of his neck. "The same people who hurt me. I didn't get mugged in the parking lot the other night. I got warned."

Elizabeth had set up an appointment for Todd and herself to meet with T. Clay Santos, the head of the Alumni Association. She was hoping to convince him to reinstate Todd on the basketball team. But before they'd gotten to meet him, Todd had been beaten up in the parking lot. He was sent home with a warning to stay out of the investigative business or risk a more brutal injury.

"By whom?"

"That's the sixty-four-thousand-dollar question. Correction. The ten-million-dollar question. Whoever beat me up is probably part of the same group that pumped ten million dollars into the athletics budget and mysteriously disbursed it. But basically, we can't prove anything. We'll never be able to prove anything until we find somebody who's involved and willing to talk to the federal authorities. So far, no luck."

"What about Mark Gathers? When you talked to him, did you tell him you suspected point shaving?"

Todd shook his head. "No. I just told him I was trying to clear things up and get us back on the team. He said he'd come down and talk to us. But he sounded a little wary. It wouldn't surprise me if he changed his mind."

He put his hand over hers. It was a small hand but a strong one, and Todd marveled again at her physical perfection. Gin-Yung's hair always hung straight and formed a line just above her shoulders. Her nose was perfectly shaped and in just the right place. Her eyes were just the right size. Her feet were just the right shape. Todd loved everything about her.

Gin-Yung was peering at him with an expression of captured fascination, but it was clear that it wasn't his charms that piqued her interest. It was her intense curiosity about what was going on. The thought was so ego deflating Todd actually laughed out loud.

"What's so funny?" she asked.

"You," he answered. He leaned forward and kissed her nose. "Stay out of it, please."

He saw her eyes wander toward Elizabeth, and he could practically hear the wheels in her busy mind crank into overdrive.

"Yes. We will be spending a lot of time together. But I'll be thinking of you the whole time."

She shook her head. "That's not good enough."

"What do you want?"

"I just spent two and a half hours racking my brains, giving you and Elizabeth stats and figures and dates and scores. I want to play too. I want to be involved."

"You can't."

"Why not?"

"Because I'm asking you not to. Please, Gin-Yung." He kissed her cheek. "Please," he repeated. "You've done a great job of helping, but now the rest is up to us. I'll start making calls tomorrow, tracking down some of the guys who've disappeared over the last few years. Elizabeth will try to get us another appointment with Santos. Beyond that, there's nothing else to do at this point."

"You still need me," she said with a smug smile.

"No doubt about it," he murmured, giving her hand a romantic squeeze.

"I mean, you need me on this investigation. You still don't know who mugged you, do you?"

He frowned. "No. How could I know that?"

She shook her head, and her gleaming black hair rippled. "Sometimes you're so dense. I can't believe you don't see it. It's so obvious. According to Dr. Beal, the Alumni Association is blocking your reinstatement. The day you have an appointment with the head of the Alumni Association, you get jumped in the parking lot. T. Clay Santos may be the head of the Alumni Association, but ten bucks says he's also the head of a gambling ring that's financing a point-shaving scheme out of the SVU athletics budget." She blew on her nails and pretended to buff them on the shoulder of her blazer. "Still think you don't need me anymore?"

Todd's jaw dropped, and he felt as if somebody had just turned a spotlight on a shadowy landscape. She was right. It was incredibly obvious.

But he was right too. This was dangerous territory. Todd smoothed her hair with his hand and looked deep into her dark eyes. "I do need you," he said softly. "Which is why I want you to stay safe. And the only way to stay safe is to stay out of it."

"I will, but only on one condition."

"What's that?"

"You give me an exclusive interview when this is all over."

"You have my word." He leaned toward her. "And I'll seal it with a kiss."

Chapter Four

"Can you believe it? Lila and Bruce are moving in together!" Isabella Ricci said.

"Yeah. They found an amazing beach-front condo. I'm helping them move this afternoon," Jessica told the group of her sorority sisters. Jessica had grown up with both Bruce and Lila and was now prepared to deflect questions about them from the group.

Jessica and her sorority sisters were sitting at a long breakfast table in the cafeteria, laughing and joking and teasing each other over coffee and pastries.

At one end of the table Jessica's best friend, Isabella Ricci, sat dressed in her customary funky high fashion—black tights, black silk sweater, and a sheer scarf draped around her shoulders. Her long dark hair was pulled back in a ponytail, and she wore two different-colored asymmetrical sea glass earrings.

The outfit was a bit much for a regular day of college classes, but Isabella could carry it off.

"Do you think it's such a smart idea for them? After all, Lila can be a bit difficult to handle on a full-time basis," Denise Waters said. She was sitting next to Isabella. Her small, perfect figure was completely hidden in baggy overalls worn over something made of white cotton flannel with little yellow flowers on it.

Jessica wondered if it was her nightgown. Denise was perfectly capable of rolling out of bed, putting her overalls on over her nightgown, and going to class. As with Isabella, sheer force of personality made it seem wonderfully stylish, individual, and sophisticated.

Next to Denise sat Alison Quinn, the snooty vice president of the Thetas and Jessica's archenemy. As usual, Alison was busy giving Jessica dirty looks across the table and buttering up Magda, the president of the sorority.

Most of the time Jessica enjoyed the sisterhood, friendship, rivalries, and fashion parade that made their sorority breakfasts fun. But this morning her thoughts were a million miles away. She wished they would change the subject so she could think in peace. "I don't know whether it'll last or not," Jessica said. "But let's talk about somebody else."

"I know, did I tell you guys about two of my friends who moved in together . . ." Isabella began.

45

Jessica sipped her coffee slowly, thinking of Professor Miles. Louis. She shivered happily at the memory of his touch . . . the memory of his tender kiss . . . She tuned out the conversation around her and continued her delicious daydream.

She had a heavy-lidded, sleepy feeling that had nothing to do with lack of rest. What Jessica felt was the sweet ache of love.

The sweetest ache she had ever felt. *Love hurts,* went the repeating refrain to one of her favorite songs. She'd always agreed. Love did hurt. She had been hurt by love more than once. But now the words had a whole different meaning. Because this hurt, this ache, felt good. It was the kind of ache she felt after a hard workout. It was a pain that reminded her that she was young and healthy and alive.

A movement of Alison's head caught Jessica's attention. Alison tossed her thin brown hair off her shoulders and pressed her lips together at the same time.

There was a flurry of commotion on Alison's side of the table as everybody reacted at once and began rearranging themselves. Kimberly sat up straighter, Tina tweaked at her spiky bangs, and Magda delicately wiped a dab of egg from the corner of her mouth with her little finger. "Isn't he the cutest professor you've ever seen?" she said under her breath.

Jessica turned to see who was getting the big reaction, and she couldn't help but smile.

46

Louis.

"Professor Miles!" Alison called out, fluttering her perfectly manicured fingers in his direction. "Come sit with us."

Louis smiled at the group of girls as he approached. He put his tray down on their table and didn't see Jessica until he was halfway into his seat. His face flushed, and he practically dropped the tray in his confusion. Coffee spilled in every direction.

"Oh, here, let me help," Alison said, shoving napkins at him.

"Let me get you another coffee." Tina rushed to get him another cup.

Jessica lowered her eyes and bit back a smile. It was obvious they all had crushes on him. If they only knew. If they had any idea at all what had gone on between them yesterday . . .

"Sit down, Professor Miles," Denise said with a big grin. "And tell us how many openings you have left in your course."

All the girls laughed, and so did Professor Miles. He gave Denise a friendly smile and glanced around the table. "I'd love to see all of you in my class, but you'll have to wait until next semester. We're too far into the term for you to catch up on all the work now."

Tina put a cup of coffee down in front of him, and he smiled his thanks.

"Could we sit in and audit a lecture?" Alison asked brightly. "That way we can see if we like the subject as much as we like you."

47

The girls giggled, and Louis grinned and blushed again. "I'd be flattered to see any of you in my class," he said in a funny, dignified voice. "Please drop by anytime."

"Oh, we will," Alison purred. She finished with an elaborate flutter of her eyelashes.

Jessica saw Isabella and Denise exchange an amused glance. Alison Quinn wasn't the most subtle flirt in the world, and her obvious maneuvering wasn't lost on anybody at the table, including Louis.

Louis blushed to the roots of his hair. She was obviously making him self-conscious, but he took it in good humor and managed to address Alison with a composed face. "I'd ask Jessica all about the class before you decide to join us. I'm a pretty hard taskmaster. If you don't believe me, ask her about the essay I assigned her."

Startled to hear her name on his lips, Jessica practically dropped her own coffee cup. To cover her confusion, she took a big gulp of the hot coffee. It was so hot that it scalded her mouth. She swallowed and moaned loudly.

"Don't be overly dramatic," Louis teased. "I'm not that bad." His eyes met hers and crinkled in an intimate smile. He was flirting with her under their very noses—trying to amuse her and himself.

He was playing a dangerous game. Jessica realized that Louis Miles had absolutely no idea who he was dealing with when it came to Alison Quinn and her friends. He had no concept of the amount of gossip a few suspicious minds around Theta house could cause.

The girls collapsed in giggles, and Jessica could feel herself blushing. *My feelings are written all over my face,* she thought in a sudden panic. *All I need is for Alison or one of the other girls to get wind of what's happened and I'll never hear the end of it. And neither will Louis. I'd better get out of here.*

Jessica quickly reached down and found her purse underneath her seat. She picked up her books and tossed her hair off the shoulder of her hot pink sweater. "I've got to go," she said, making a show of looking at her watch.

"Where?" Denise demanded, taking a large forkful of cheese pastry from Isabella's plate. "You said you were free until third class," Denise continued thickly, her face puzzled.

Jessica froze, like a deer caught in the headlights of an oncoming car. She looked around the table. It seemed as if every face was staring at her with an unusual degree of interest. Louis's eyes were fixed on the saucer beneath his cup. *I'm getting totally paranoid,* Jessica thought. *Nobody knows anything because there's nothing to know.*

Unless somebody saw us in the car yesterday, the paranoid side of her brain argued.

Her heart gave an uncomfortable thump. Was it possible? Could somebody have been out on the sidewalk in the torrential storm? Had Magda or Tina or Kimberly caught a glimpse of Jessica locked in a passionate embrace with Professor Louis Miles?

No, she decided, pushing her worries away. Nobody could have seen. "I just forgot I have to do something . . ." she said quickly. "In the library. I have to return a book." Refusing to meet his eyes, she turned and hurried from the cafeteria, practically running. She couldn't get out of there fast enough.

Louis laughed at something one of the girls said, but the laugh was automatic. He hadn't really heard what she'd said. In spite of his determination not to watch Jessica, his eyes had followed her all the way across the cafeteria and through the plate-glass exit doors.

They were still focused on her now as she walked out onto the quadrangle. He noticed she was going in the opposite direction from the library.

He understood why she'd left. He'd been on the verge of leaving himself when he realized it was impossible to be near her and not acknowledge his feelings for her.

But once she had announced that she was leaving, Louis felt he had to stay behind for another few minutes to curtail any suspicions. Not that any of these girls had a clue about his feelings for Jessica.

"Professor Miles," one of them asked, interrupting his thoughts. The tall one. The one who looked like a model.

"I'm sorry," he said, giving her an apologetic smile. "Tell me your name, please."

"It's Isabella. Isabella Ricci."

"And I'm Alison Quinn," said the girl with the straight brown hair. The one who had invited him over to this table in the first place. Louis gave her a polite but remote smile. He'd met her type on every campus and in every class. She was the girl who was determined to flirt with her teachers. And she could easily become a pest if given the least amount of encouragement.

"Miss Quinn and Miss Ricci," he said, observing the formalities in order to pleasantly remind them that he was not here to play with them. "Tell me how all of you know each other. Are you in the same dorm?"

"We're all members of the same sorority," the small one in the overalls explained. "We're Thetas. And we meet here for breakfast every Tuesday."

The girls chattered on.

Louis remained seated until he felt he could reasonably leave. In the meantime, he tried hard to dispel any thoughts about Jessica and to remind himself of the impossibility of a relationship.

This was her world. Her reality. It was a world of sorority sisters, parties, dates with guys her own age, and carefree friendships.

Louis had no right to draw Jessica into the hell that had become his world. Another wave of blazing anger rose in his chest, and he put his water glass down gently. Afraid he'd smash it down on

51

the table and break it like he did the coffee mug the night before.

The anger subsided and was replaced with bitter regret. He'd sell his soul for a different reality. He'd trade his life for the right to walk out of this cafeteria next to Jessica, her hand held tightly in his.

He wanted to take her out to dinner and look at her beautiful face across a candlelit table. He wanted to see the million expressions that crossed her face in a nanosecond and take her to all the strange and exotic restaurants he loved.

Then they could walk down the street, look in shop windows, and wander around, searching for just the right place to have coffee. She would turn her face up to look at him, and they would kiss under the glow of a streetlamp as they waited for a light to change.

Oh, Jessica, his heart ached. *If only you knew how much I care.* But he had no right to tell her. He'd already taken a dangerous chance. They'd been seen once already. On the beach. His heart began to pound. He'd checked the rearview mirror several times yesterday. There had been no car parked behind them. And as far as he knew, no one had been on the sidewalk beside the car. But there had been a space of time when his attention had been diverted. When he'd been lost in Jessica's lips. Could someone have walked up and seen them? Involuntarily his free hand flew to his brow.

"Professor Miles! Are you all right?" The tall one, Isabella, stared at him, her brows raised in concern. "Is something wrong?"

He realized that his coffee cup was half dangling from the fingers of one hand while his other hand massaged his forehead.

He put down the cup and smiled. "I'm sorry. I was trying to remember what I'd done with some papers, and I just realized I left them in my trunk." Louis glanced at his watch. "If I hurry, I'll barely have time to go back to my car and get them before class. It was nice meeting all of you. Excuse me." He could still hear them calling out their good-byes as he headed for the exit.

Mark Gathers stepped over the pile of lumber and construction materials that littered the back entrance to the student union. Odd. Lots of mess. No workmen. The whole area had the unattended look of an on-again, off-again project to which no one was committed. Tools were scattered in a haphazard fashion, and sheets of particle board and insulation material were soaking wet.

He picked his way carefully through the mess and entered the building. As soon as he stepped into the cafeteria, Mark spotted Isabella Ricci, Denise Waters, Alison Quinn, and a bunch of the other Thetas sitting on the far side of the cafeteria. Alexandra Rollins, his ex-girlfriend, wasn't at the table with them. He didn't know whether he was relieved or disappointed.

"Mark!" A heavy hand grabbed his sleeve and pulled him to a stop. Ben Alsup, an old friend from the basketball team, grinned up at him from his chair. "Mark Gathers! I can't believe it," he cried happily. "What are you doing here?"

Mark shook the hand that was offered. "I had some business in the area, so I thought I'd take a walk around campus and see if everything looked the same."

Ben gestured across the table at a guy Mark had never seen before. "Mark, this is Tony Shear, my new roommate."

Mark smiled and held out his hand to shake. But Tony didn't smile back. Nor did he extend his hand. Tony removed his jacket from the back of his chair and gave Mark a cold look. "I've gotta go, Ben. I'll see you later." He started to stand.

"Tony!" Ben exclaimed in an embarrassed voice.

Mark's hand curled into an angry ball. For two cents, he'd love to punch Tony right in the mouth. Instead he put a hand on Tony's shoulder and pushed him back down into his seat. "Don't bother. I'm leaving."

Mark began walking toward the exit, refusing to look left or right. "Mark, wait. Hold on a second." Behind him, Ben hurried to catch up.

Mark turned and raised his brows, bored. He didn't need to hear Ben apologize for his friend's idiotic behavior. "Forget it, Ben. It's happened before. It'll happen again."

"Tony's just a little . . ." Ben shrugged. "He's a very principled guy."

"Meaning what? That I'm not?" Mark asked impatiently.

Ben held up his hands. "Hey! I always said you got a raw deal. You were one of the best players I've ever seen. When you got kicked off the team, I wrote a letter to the newspaper and the administration protesting it. I wrote one about Wilkins too. You ever see him?"

Mark looked up and shoved his hands in his pockets. He wasn't going to explain that he was here at the request of Todd Wilkins. Mark knew that Todd had gone through some bad times after they got kicked off the team—drinking, dropping out, legal problems. But according to Todd, all that had been straightened out, and he was getting his life together. He needed Mark's help, and he thought he could help Mark too.

Mark cast a glance in Tony's direction and decided Todd was probably nuts. You couldn't fight public opinion any more than you could fight a vigilante reporter like Elizabeth Wakefield. She'd gotten mad at Todd for breaking up with her, and she'd taken it out on the whole athletics department—making a big stink over a few perks. She'd ruined Todd's career . . . and his.

I'm wasting my time here, Mark thought. "I'll see you around," he said curtly to Ben.

"How long are you going to be here?" Ben called after him. "Maybe we could get together."

Mark didn't answer as his eyes scanned the cafeteria. He saw a lot of familiar faces. Some smiled, but most went carefully blank.

Man! Mark Gathers, onetime superstar of the SVU basketball team, was now a first-class pariah. How did Wilkins stand this day in and day out? Maybe it wore off if you stuck around long enough. But Mark hadn't bothered to find out. When he'd been kicked off the team and had his scholarship revoked, he'd bailed. He'd thrown everything he had into his Explorer and gone to L.A. to try to make it in the pros. Unfortunately he hadn't made it. One scout had said he just didn't have the seasoning yet. He needed another year or so in the NCAA leagues.

But that wasn't possible. He was out of college ball, and the only job he'd been able to land in sports was selling hot dogs and T-shirts during the games. It was pretty humiliating. He'd been miserable when Todd Wilkins had tracked him down.

I don't need these people, he decided again. They'd treated him like dirt. They'd ground him up in their system and plowed him under. Well, it was their loss, and he didn't owe this school anything.

Mark reached into his pocket for his car keys and headed for the visitors' parking lot. There was no sense in staying. He'd call Todd from the highway somewhere and tell him something came up. He'd answered all the questions about the recruiting scandal he was going to.

His black cowboy boots made half moons in the soft, post-rainy turf of the quadrangle. To his left, Mark saw the administration building, where he'd been so warmly greeted by the school officials and alumni when he had arrived for his freshman year.

Behind it, he saw the athletics complex.

It gave him a funny feeling in the pit of his stomach—regret and rage all mixed up together. Mark had walked around with that feeling for a long time after his suspension. Little by little, he'd put it behind him.

Coming back to SVU brought all those old feelings rushing back, and he didn't like it. Mark quickened his step. *The sooner I get out of here, the better.*

A familiar head of coppery curls on the other side of the parking lot brought him to a skidding stop.

Alex!

He watched her shift her book bag from one arm to the other and couldn't help admiring the shape of her slim hips and long legs as she hurried along the walk that led to the student union. *I'm an idiot!* he thought angrily, climbing into his Explorer.

The engine roared and he sped away, refusing to look in the rearview mirror back at good old SVU.

Chapter Five

"Please keep your tests facedown until they have all been handed out." Professor Stark moved up and down the aisle, handing out the examinations.

Professor Stark gave one to Winston, and he obediently turned it over and laid it on the desk. Winston's palms were sweating, and he wiped his hands on the knees of his jeans.

"I want you all to relax." Professor Stark gave the last test to a redheaded boy in the back row and returned to the front of the class. "This test is not easy, but it's not impossible. .Not if you have studied the material and are adequately prepared."

Winston exchanged a nervous smile with the blond girl who sat next to him, then he lifted his pencil to his lips and began to chew the eraser.

"Once the test begins, you will have fifty minutes to complete it. If you hit a question you cannot answer, move on to the next one. Go back to the difficult ones later. If you finish early, please bring your test up to my desk, put it down, and leave the room as quietly as possible."

Winston's heart was hammering inside his thin chest. What if this wasn't the same test as the one he'd stolen? What if Professor Stark had counted the number of copies he'd made and noticed that one was missing? If so, he might have created an entirely new exam last night in an attempt to foil a would-be cheater.

All of a sudden something lodged in Winston's throat, and he began to cough violently.

The blond girl next to him reached over to pat him on the back, but it didn't help. It just made things worse. Horrified, Winston realized that he'd bitten off the end of his eraser and swallowed it.

"Mr. Egbert, would you like to leave the room and get some water?"

Winston nodded. Still coughing, he lurched from his seat and into the hall. He practically fell on the water fountain outside the door and splashed himself in the face a couple of times while he fumbled with the handle.

Two or three splats later, he managed to gulp down enough water to push the eraser out of his windpipe and down into his digestive track.

It wasn't a great way to start the day, but his digestive tract had seen things far more exotic than a pencil eraser. The thought of crunchy doodle bugs, cool marbles, and a dollar fifty's worth of buffalo nickels brought back fond memories of his childhood.

Snap out of it. This is no time for fond memories, he told himself sternly. He was about to commit the ultimate college crime—cheating.

Winston shook his head to clear it. Beads of sweat flew from his brow in every direction.

Maybe he should call the whole thing off. He could tell Professor Stark he had suddenly succumbed to some kind of strange rubber allergy. That way, he could take a makeup exam later.

Makeup exams were always different from the original exams. If he took a makeup exam, it wouldn't be the same test he had memorized last night.

Yeah, that's what he would do. Winston Egbert was a class clown and a sometimes irresponsible student, but he wasn't a cheater.

At least not yet.

He still had his honor and his self-respect.

Winston put his hand on the doorknob, but then froze. Hey, wait a minute. What good were honor and self-respect going to do him when he was miles away from the love of his life?

Denise Waters was Marilyn Monroe, Joan of Arc, Margaret Thatcher, and Helen of Troy all wrapped up in one neat, petite package. Did the rules matter when it came to being with the woman he loved?

Winston squared his shoulders and sailed back into the classroom with bravado to spare. He even gave the nervous blonde a cocky wink as he took his seat and flipped over the test.

Eureka! It was the same test—word for word.

Winston pulled his spare pencil from his back-pack and began to scribble answers to the familiar problem sets.

Todd drummed his fingers on the desk, waiting for someone to answer the phone. He swiveled rest-lessly in his desk chair, looking around his dorm room at the sports posters on the wall. It had been a late-semester dorm assignment, and he didn't have a roommate—which was perfectly fine with him. He liked his privacy these days, and having no roommate meant he could be on the phone all day and not worry about being overheard. He was spending all his free time working his way down the list of ex-players he and Elizabeth had put together.

The phone continued ringing, and Todd swiv-eled again, looking out the window and wonder-ing how Elizabeth was doing at her end. When she'd heard Gin-Yung's theory, she became com-pletely determined to get an appointment with Santos, even if she had to call his office every five minutes.

"Hello?"

Todd's mind had been so preoccupied, the voice on the other end of the line startled him. He had to refer to Gin-Yung's list to remind him who he was calling. "May I speak to . . . uh . . . Jimmy McFarland?"

"Speaking," the voice at the other end said. Todd had tracked down Jimmy's phone number with the help of the fraternity files and an operator in Fresno.

"Is this the Jimmy McFarland who played ball for SVU a couple of years ago?"

There was a long pause. "Who wants to know?" the voice shot back in a playful comeback. The tone was light, but Todd thought he heard a slight note of antagonism.

Todd changed the phone from his right ear to his left and picked up his pencil to take notes in case Jimmy said anything he needed to write down. "This is Todd Wilkins at SVU," Todd answered.

"What can I do for you, Todd?"

"I was wondering if you'd answer a question for me."

"I will if I can."

"When you were playing for SVU, did anybody ever offer you money to drop the ball?"

The hang up was abrupt and very loud. Todd jerked his head away from the phone and blew out his breath. It wasn't an entirely unexpected reaction. Jimmy McFarland's hang up wasn't anything he could put in the bank or take to a district attorney, but it answered the question. Todd checked the little box he'd drawn by Jimmy's name and began looking through the L.A. phone book for Paul Brittain's number.

*   *   *

Twenty miles out of town, Mark Gathers pulled off the road and stopped the Explorer. He stared at the traffic that sped to and from campus along the double lanes of the highway.

The image of Alex in her slim-fitting jeans lingered in his mind. She looked fantastic. He'd really missed her.

He hadn't treated her well during the fiasco of the sports scandal. He'd been too angry. Afterward he'd been too macho to apologize.

"I'm such a loser," he yelled to himself. Mark threw the engine into gear and made a U-turn, heading back toward Sweet Valley University. His mind went around and around—thinking about Alex, thinking about Todd, thinking about Ben and his friend and all the cold, unforgiving faces that had stared at him in the cafeteria.

He still wasn't sure whether or not he wanted to cooperate with Wilkins. But he had one or two things he wanted to settle before leaving Sweet Valley County for good.

"May I speak to Chuck Hooper, please," Todd asked.

It was his fifth phone call. He'd been unable to reach Paul Brittain. His mother had said he was fishing somewhere in the Caribbean.

Perry Taft's mother had burst into tears and said she hadn't seen Perry in three years.

Clint Stein, like Jimmy McFarland, had simply

hung up on Todd, refusing to give his address or say where he was living.

"Just a second," a deep voice said on the other end of the line. "Let me see if I can find him."

Todd sat forward and rubbed the back of his aching neck while he listened to whoever had answered the phone yell for Chuck at the top of his voice. This time, Todd was going to try a different tack—try to get an address and then look him up in person if possible.

Somebody lowered the volume of the loud rock and roll blasting at the other end of the line and picked up the phone. "Hello?"

"Is this Chuck Hooper?"

"This is Chuck. Who's calling?"

"This is Todd Wilkins from SVU."

"Oh? Do I know you?"

"I don't think so."

"I don't really keep up with anybody from SVU. How did you find me?"

Todd chuckled. "You sound like you're in hiding."

There was no answering chuckle on the other end.

"I called your house, and your mom gave me the number of a friend in Seattle. Then your friend in Seattle told me I could reach you here. Where is here, by the way?"

"Why are you calling me?" Chuck asked abruptly, ignoring the question.

"Fund-raising," Todd answered quickly.

"We're doing a telethon and contacting all the alumni."

"Oh," Chuck said, sounding relieved. "Oh, I see." He laughed. "You sure went to a lot of trouble to track me down."

"Yeah, well, what the heck? It's on the school's phone bill, and I like playing private detective."

"Private detective?" Chuck repeated slowly.

"That's a joke," Todd said, sitting forward and listening intently. "I just mean I like the challenge of finding people and getting in touch. It's the sort of thing that keeps you occupied but doesn't get graded."

"Yeah. Right." Chuck's voice relaxed again, and Todd exhaled. Wow. This guy was really on his guard. Todd needed to proceed very carefully. "Well, um," Chuck mused, "I don't have time to talk, but I guess you could put me down for twenty dollars."

"Great. Great!" Todd said, reaching for his pencil. "What we'll do is send you a pledge bill and you just send it back with your check or money order or whatever. What's your address?"

Quickly Todd jotted down the address in Fulton, a town about seventy miles away. "Great, Chuck. Thanks a lot."

"No problem," Chuck replied.

Todd hung up the phone and smiled. He'd call Elizabeth and tell her they had a lead. The phone rang, and Todd eagerly answered it, hoping it was Elizabeth. "Guess what?" he said.

"What?" a deep male voice asked in an expressionless voice.

"I'm sorry. I thought you were someone else. This is Todd Wilkins—who is this?"

"A friend," the voice answered. "With a message."

Todd sat up straighter. "Which is?"

"You ask too many questions. Knock it off." The caller hung up with a loud click.

Todd sat back and bit his lip. The phone rang again, and he picked it up. "Hello?"

"We're in luck," Elizabeth said.

"How so?"

"I just got a call from Mr. Santos's secretary. We have an appointment tomorrow morning."

"Great," Todd said. "I got a phone call too."

"From Mark Gathers?"

"No. From somebody who wants me to stop asking questions."

There was a long silence at the other end of the phone. Then, "What do you think that means?"

"I think it means we're getting close to some answers. And it's making somebody very nervous. And tomorrow morning, we'll find out if that somebody is T. Clay Santos."

Chapter Six

"Where do you want this, Lila?" Jessica groaned. "Quick! Make a decision!" The heavy cardboard box began slipping from her arms, and her knees sagged. It was late afternoon and this was the tenth box she'd carried up the steep condo stairs from her Jeep. The muscles in her legs felt like rubber.

Bruce Patman raced over. "Here, Jessica, give it to me. That's way too heavy for you to carry."

"Now you tell me," she joked, gratefully handing off the load to Bruce. "What's in here, anyway?" She straightened the shoulder of her white cotton knit sweater. The wide boat neck had slipped halfway down her arm, revealing a golden shoulder. It was the same tawny color as the section of her stomach that showed above the waist of her faded low riders.

"My trophies." Bruce opened the lid and removed a heavy urn with the figure of a tennis player mounted on the top. He carried it to the mantel and placed it over the fireplace. "How about here, Lila? What do you think?"

But Lila Fowler was too busy counting the boxes of china that had been delivered that morning from Benson's, Sweet Valley's most expensive china and crystal shop. "Bruce," she complained. "I ordered place settings for twenty, and I think they only sent eighteen."

Bruce shrugged. "So call them and tell them to send the rest ASAP." He went over to where she sat on the floor and bent down to kiss her cheek. "Tell them Lila Fowler and Bruce Patman have officially moved into their romantic beach-front love nest. They're planning a big party and they want the works."

Jessica smiled. It was hard to believe, but Lila and Bruce actually made a cute couple.

Lila Fowler had been Jessica's best friend since grammar school, and she had always been the richest girl in town. In high school Lila had a wardrobe like a movie star, a bedroom like a stage set, and a life like a princess.

But money hadn't been able to shield her from a terrible and appalling tragedy.

While Jessica, Elizabeth, Alex, Bruce, and Winston had been enrolling in freshman classes at SVU, Lila had gone to Europe and impulsively married a young, handsome Italian count, Tisiano di Mondicci.

Tisiano had died in an accident only months after their wedding. Heartbroken, Lila had returned to SVU and tried to pick up her life where she had left off.

Surprisingly, miraculously, she had fallen head over heels in love with Bruce Patman. After years of arguing, bickering, competing, and despising each other, they had turned out to be soul mates.

Bruce was perfect for Lila because he was just as rich and pampered as she was. Lila had always been spoiled, and Jessica had stopped resenting it a long time ago. It was part of Lila's charm.

Bruce had been raised with a lot of money, but it was only after arriving at college that he had inherited a huge trust fund that put him on an equal financial footing with Lila.

Jessica watched them brush their lips together and giggle as they pulled one expensive item from the box after another.

She enjoyed seeing Lila happy again. If Jessica couldn't be happy herself, it was good to know that Lila was. And it was nice that the object of her love loved her back. They had no hesitation about letting the world know how they felt about each other. No fears about jobs. No embarrassment about whether or not their feelings for each other were "appropriate."

An expensive glass dropped from Lila's hand and shattered as Bruce's kiss became more passionate. In true Lila-Bruce fashion, neither one of them paid the least bit of attention, and their embrace grew even more heated.

"I'll get another box from the Jeep," Jessica announced, backing away to give the couple privacy. But she couldn't help chuckling as she descended the stairs of the beach house. She doubted that either one had heard her. *Better give them a few minutes alone,* she thought, wandering onto the beach and staring out at the waves.

The sound of the booming surf rose and fell like the breathing of a human being. Jessica kicked off her shoes and walked to the water's edge, letting the water lap up against her toes. It was warm, and she couldn't resist walking in a few inches deeper.

She bent her head and hugged herself. To the left and half a mile down the beach was Louis's condo. Jessica closed her eyes and tried to imagine him standing on his deck, watching her.

I won't turn around, she vowed. *I won't turn and look. No matter what, I'm not going to look toward his house.*

She turned deliberately in the opposite direction and began walking through the water, kicking up a little spray and trying to look nonchalant.

Suddenly she felt something tingle down the back of her spine. Someone was watching her.

Louis was home. He was on the deck. He was looking at her. She just knew it.

She turned and stared down the beach, with her pulse racing. She was right. Louis stood out on the deck, wearing a white cotton shirt that billowed in the breeze.

I'll just stroll in his direction, she thought, fighting hard to keep from breaking into a run. *I'll just walk by, wave, and then keep on walking.* She stared determinedly down at her feet, making a great show of looking at shells and even stopping once or twice to examine something on the beach.

Finally, after what seemed like an eternity, she was in front of his house. Slowly, casually, Jessica turned her head toward it, as if she were just happening to glance up.

When she did, the sand shifted beneath her feet and she swayed, trying hard to catch her breath.

Louis was standing on the deck, but he wasn't alone. There was a woman with him. Actually, she was plastered against his chest. Her arms were woven around his waist and her face was buried in his shoulder. Her long black curls flew out, half covering his face. He lifted his hand to brush them away, and his eyes met Jessica's.

He looked startled to see her, and Jessica stepped away, feeling physically ill. She turned and began to run back toward Lila's condo. Her bare feet pounded the wet sand and sent up a spray of water that drenched the legs of her jeans.

Tears streamed down her cheeks, and she sobbed into the wind. No wonder he didn't want a relationship with her. He had a relationship with someone else.

Her stomach lurched. How could he have kissed her like that in the car? Were all her instincts so off that she couldn't detect the lie in his touch?

71

Why hadn't he told her the truth? Why did he have to make up stupid excuses about his job?

Jessica scooped up her shoes from the water's edge and ran up the stairs of Lila's condo. She paused outside the door and took some deep breaths to bring her shuddering sobs to a halt. When she felt like she was back in control, she walked inside.

Bruce and Lila sat on the living room floor, happily arguing over wallpaper samples. "Jess!" Lila cried, holding up a square of paper with an astronomy theme. "Isn't this the ugliest wallpaper you've ever seen?" Clusters of white spots representing constellations dotted a navy blue background.

Bruce let out a bark of protest. "Your taste is in your mouth, Lila. Back me up here, Jessica. This wallpaper is amazing. Very contemporary. Very hip. It's cosmic. It's New Age. It's . . ." He snapped his fingers. "Give me a word, Jessica."

Jessica did her best to smile, but the muscles in her face were so tight her whole mouth began to tremble. "I think it's . . ." Her voice disappeared into a high, thin squeak, and her hands flew to her eyes.

"Jessica? Is something wrong?" Lila asked.

Jessica shook her head. "No. It's the wind. I got a bunch of sand in my eyes. I'd better wash it out." She went into the bathroom, closed the door, and pressed the towel to her mouth to muffle the sound of her sobs.

*   *   *

72

Louis ran barefoot up the beach, his torn shirt hanging open and his baggy khakis rolled up to the knee. Down the beach, over some of the dunes, he could see Jessica's Jeep parked beneath the condo her friends were moving into. *Jessica's still here,* Louis thought thankfully. *She hasn't left yet.*

He'd had to wait until it was safe to come after her. He'd thought his unwelcome visitor would never leave. But finally, after what had seemed like hours, she had departed. And as usual, she had left in a rage—screaming threats before she got into her car and screeched away, going who knew where. She had an almost supernatural ability to appear and disappear.

The door to the condo opened. He heard Jessica shout good-bye as she descended the stairs with a set of keys clutched in her hand.

"Jessica!" he called out.

When she saw him, she broke into a run.

"Jessica, wait!"

"Go away," she yelled.

He closed the distance between them easily and grabbed her upper arm, yanking her to a stop.

"Let me go," she yelled, trying to twist her arm away.

But he tightened his grip and pulled her from the drive, roughly dragging her behind him until they were hidden behind two high, sloping dunes.

She tried to run away again, but he pulled her tightly against his chest. The force of it knocked them both to the ground, and he fell on top of her.

"Get off me," she demanded through gritted teeth.

"Please don't run away."

"Let me up."

"Please don't run away," he repeated. "I know you're upset. And I don't blame you. You want an explanation."

"No, I don't," she shouted. "You're going to tell me that you don't owe me an explanation because there's nothing between us. I can't stand to hear you say it."

"Then I won't say it," he said, tightening his grasp on her wrists. He leaned over her and kissed her with more passion and intensity than he had before, even in the car. He felt her arms go slack and then rise to encircle his shoulders.

In the privacy of the valley between the high dunes and the tall grass, Louis did his best to dispel, once and for all, any doubts she might have had about his feelings for her.

Moments later her fingers trailed down the back of his neck, and he shivered.

"Ticklish?" she teased with a languid smile.

"No," he said shortly. He drew his head away and lifted his face.

"Is something the matter?"

"Shhhh," he warned.

His nostrils flared slightly and he felt Jessica stiffen. She sat up. "Louis. What's the matter?"

He put his finger to her lips. "No one can know," he whispered. "No one, Jessica."

Her eyes searched his, puzzled. "Because of your job?"

He paused briefly. "Yes," he said. "Because of my job."

But the pause was too long. He knew it from her face.

"It's not just your job," she said, her eyes beginning to flash dangerously. "It's her, isn't it? Who is she?"

Louis dropped his head, and his mind began to race. How did he explain what was inexplicable? How could he explain what was illogical, irrational, and so intensely sick and twisted it would take hours?

He gazed at Jessica's face. It was young and fresh. But it was etched slightly with pain—like his own. She'd said she'd been married. Did an unhappy life experience like that prepare a person to understand a misery so deep and disturbing that it permeated one's every waking moment?

Her face was expectant, vulnerable, and frightened. She was afraid of being hurt, and he was afraid for her. Louis needed to protect her. And that meant not taking any chances.

A breeze blew gently past, and his nostrils flared again. Did he smell roses? Was it his imagination or was the cloying, heavy scent really there? "Come on," he said. He scrambled up, pulling her to her feet. "You have to leave."

"Louis!" she protested. "What . . ."

"Go. You have to go now."

"But I don't want to go. I want to talk about this. If we're going to work this out, you've got to tell me wh—"

"Jessica," he interrupted, "if you care anything at all about me, just do what I ask." He half pulled, half dragged her toward the drive. When they reached her Jeep, he opened the door and pushed her inside so hard she practically fell into the passenger seat. "Go!" he repeated. "Leave now!"

Her young face was stunned, bewildered, and hurt by the change in his behavior. Frustrated, he placed his hands on either side of her face. "Jessica. I will explain. Or at least I'll try to explain. I promise. But not now. I can't right now. So please go," he said softly. "I'll call you," he promised.

"When?" she asked, her blue-green eyes searching his green ones.

"Tonight," he said.

"Promise me."

"Go!" he shouted.

She hesitated only a moment, then she nodded and started the engine. The tires crunched on the oyster shell drive that led to the long beach road that wove in and out of the dunes.

Louis raced to the top of the highest dune behind an empty condo and watched the red Jeep as it disappeared into the distance.

"Oh, no," he whispered. His hands grew cold and his throat tightened with fear. Far away, about a mile down the beach, he saw a female figure standing atop another dune. She, too, was watching the red Jeep.

Chapter Seven

"Bruce!" Lila chortled. "How many tennis trophies do you have?"

Bruce arranged yet another trophy on the mantel and stood back to admire the effect. "Let me put it this way—we may have to build two or three more fireplaces to get enough mantel space."

"I have a few things I'd like to put on the mantel myself." She flopped down onto the cheap couch that had come with the condo and put her feet up on the plastic faux marble coffee table. Her perfectly manicured nails smoothed the silk lounging outfit she'd put on as soon as they were alone—peach silk pajama slacks with a matching, man-tailored silk shirt.

Bruce joined her on the couch, sitting down very close. "Oh? Like what?" He put his arm around her.

"Like the antique vase that I ordered this morning." She giggled.

Bruce leaned down and kissed the top of her head. "Expensive?"

"Obscenely." She put her arms around him, and her lips hovered seductively close to his. "This is our first home together, and I want it to be wonderful and lavish and romantic and special and . . ."

Bruce reached around to embrace her and accidentally kicked over the lightweight coffee table.

Lila sat forward and frowned. "First thing tomorrow, we're going furniture shopping. I want this junk out of here as soon as possible. I want us to have some nice stuff." She looked up, admiring the high white ceiling and the elaborately carved molding. Every architectural detail of the condo's interior was expensive and stylish. The fireplace was made of pink marble, framed in copper.

The view from the bedroom was spectacular, and the chrome-and-steel kitchen off the front hall had shutters that opened into the living room.

Lila almost purred out loud, she felt so contented. The setting was perfect. Her only area of dissatisfaction was the furniture. That was easily fixed with a little money. Fortunately, she and Bruce had plenty of it.

Bruce reached over and straightened the fallen table. "Tomorrow we'll go shopping. I say we start with breakfast at the Sweet Valley Grande. They've got a five-star dining room there. Then we'll hit some of the more exclusive antique dealers around town and get this place fixed up so that it looks great in time for the party."

Lila smiled and slumped down into the couch. "I've never been so happy in my whole life. From now on, our lives are going to be perfect."

The doorbell rang, and Bruce lifted his brows. "Are we expecting anybody?"

Lila snapped her fingers. "It's probably Benson's with the rest of the china." She ran to the door and flung it open. But much to her surprise, it wasn't a deliveryman with a securely packed box of expensive crystal—it was Mrs. Parker, their realtor.

"Ms. Fowler," Mrs. Parker cooed, "I'm so sorry to disturb you and Mr. Patman on your first evening in your new condo. But there's just one teeny-tiny little problem."

Bruce came up and stood behind her. "Problem?"

Mrs. Parker reached into the depths of her voluminous black leather bag and plucked a small piece of blue paper from the bottom. It was covered with a lot of red stamps. "Your deposit check," she said to Bruce. "I'm afraid it . . . well . . ." She laughed uncomfortably. "I'm afraid it bounced."

"Bounced!" Bruce and Lila said together.

She handed Bruce the check to examine himself. "See?"

Lila peered over Bruce's shoulder as he examined the alarming-looking notices that had been stamped all over it. RETURN! INSUFFICIENT FUNDS!

"Oh, man," Bruce said softly. "I'm sorry." He smiled weakly. "I guess I spent more this month than I realized. This has never happened to me before."

Lila nodded. "You can't believe how much stuff we've had to buy. China. Crystal. Silver. Candles. Just about everything."

Mrs. Parker smiled broadly. "Getting started is expensive, isn't it?" Her voice was extremely melodious, extremely accommodating, but extremely firm. "I'm afraid I must insist that you pay the deposit before I allow you to take possession of the condo. It's company policy. I really don't have any choice."

"Well, we'll write you another check right now. No problem, right, Lila?"

Lila nodded eagerly. "Right. We'll give you another check right now."

Mrs. Parker's broad smile widened until it reached from ear to ear. "I knew there wouldn't be any problem."

"Of course there's no problem." Bruce chuckled. He smiled nervously at Mrs. Parker, but lifted his eyebrows at Lila and jerked his head toward the kitchen.

Lila smiled in confusion. Was Bruce trying to tell her something?

Bruce jerked his head again. When she didn't respond, he took her elbow. "Would you excuse us?" he said to Mrs. Parker.

"Certainly."

Bruce led Lila into the kitchen. "So write her a check already," he whispered urgently.

"I can't," Lila protested.

"Why not?"

"I've hardly got anything left in the bank."

"What?"

"All my money is tied up with Tisiano's lawyers in Italy. There's some problem with transferring that much money out of another country. Daddy's trying to work it out, but in the meantime, all he gives me is my allowance—and it's gone."

Bruce ran a hand through his hair. "I wonder if we can put the deposit on a credit card?"

"Go ask her," Lila whispered. "I've got tons of those."

They stuck their heads out of the kitchen, and Bruce smiled broadly. "Mrs. Parker, your real-estate company doesn't by any chance take credit cards, does it?"

"I'm afraid not."

"I didn't think so."

They pulled back into the kitchen, and Bruce rubbed his forehead. "I didn't realize I'd overspent my account. I won't have any more money until next month."

"I don't understand." Lila frowned.

"I have a trust fund. That means that the principal is invested and I get to spend the interest it earns every month. If I've spent all the interest, I have to wait until the next month for more money."

"Can't you borrow from the principal?"

"No."

"Why not?" Lila demanded. "I thought you had complete control over your money."

"Almost complete control," Bruce admitted grudgingly.

"Almost?" Lila felt her temper rising. What a typical Bruce Patman move. "Bruce! Having complete control over your trust fund and almost having complete control are two different things. If you don't have complete control, it means you've got trustees."

"One trustee," he corrected.

"Who?"

"My uncle Dan."

"So you can't have any more money unless he says you can? That's terrible. Bruce, you're in as bad shape as I am."

"Hey!" Bruce barked. "At least I'm not still getting an allowance from Daddy."

"That's right," Lila retorted sarcastically. "You're getting it from Uncle Dan."

"It's not an allowance. It's my money!" he hissed.

"Then call him and tell him to give it to you." Lila yanked the phone from the wall and handed it to him.

"Lila! I can't do that."

"You can't let some trustee push you around," she insisted.

"Why not? You're letting a bunch of Italian lawyers push you around."

Lila's face clouded dangerously. "Bruce Patman. Do you want to live with me in this beautiful love nest or not?"

Bruce grabbed the phone out of her hands and began to dial decisively.

Lila smiled approvingly and leaned close so she could listen to the conversation.

"Move over," Bruce whispered. "You're taking up the whole ear part of the receiver."

"Shhh," Lila responded irritably, pushing her head even closer to his. She was determined to hear every word.

"Hello?" a querulous voice answered after four rings.

"Uncle Dan? It's Bruce. How are you doing?"

"Better than you, son," the old man cackled. "I'm not broke with a female nagging me."

Lila drew herself up angrily. "How does he know that? Has he got this place bugged?" she demanded. "And besides, I am not nagging you."

"Shhhh!" Bruce warned. He forced a chuckle and pulled nervously at the neck of his purple polo shirt with his index finger. "Well, I wouldn't describe the situation exactly that way. Listen, Uncle Dan, I'm a little short this month and . . ."

"A little short. I just got a call from your bank. Did you know you're bouncing checks all over town?"

"That's because I've moved, Uncle Dan."

"I know that. And you've moved in with some girl. I'm not stupid. What does a young man want with a complete set of silver? Nothing. Not unless there's a female around. I'm gonna tell you something, son."

"What's that?"

"I've never had any luck with women, and my advice to you is leave 'em alone. She wants your money. They all do. You're a rich young man and you've got to be on guard against fortune hunters."

"Me? A fortune hunter? What is he—nuts?" Lila hissed in outrage. "Give me that phone."

"Shhhhh!" Bruce warned again. He took a deep breath, put the phone back to his ear, and smiled ingratiatingly. Lila thrust her head against his so that she could hear. "Uncle Dan, I don't think you fully understand. Lila's not a fortune hunter. In fact, her parents are the Fowlers of Fowler Enterprises."

"Never heard of 'em, and I don't care to, either," Uncle Dan said succinctly. "Now, you listen to me, boy. My job is to make sure you don't throw your money away. And I intend to do it."

"All I'm asking is for a loan against next month's dividends."

"No can do, sonny."

"Uncle Dan! Do you realize what this means?"

"It means you can go back to Sigma house. Your room and board is paid for through the end of the semester."

"I'm a grown man, Uncle Dan. And I resent you treating me like a child."

Lila nodded briskly. "You tell him!" she whispered approvingly.

"I'm entitled to make my own decisions. I don't want to live in Sigma house. I want to live with Lila, the woman I love. The woman who loves me."

Lila smiled happily and squeezed his arm.

"Fine. If she loves you, then let her pay the rent."

Uncle Dan hung up the phone, and Lila and Bruce stared at each other. "I can't believe it," she whispered, feeling stunned. "We don't have any money."

"Think your dad would lend you some?"

Lila shook her head. "No. When I told him you and I were thinking of moving in together, he told me not to."

"What did you say?"

Lila shrugged. "Nothing. I figured I'd just do it anyway and then tell him about it later."

"Then we can't stay here!" Bruce said.

"Bruce," Lila wailed. "This is terrible. I want to live with you. I've got my heart set on it. If we can't live together I'll . . . I'll—" She broke off with a sob and collapsed against his chest.

Bruce held her close and patted her soothingly on the back. "Lila," he said tentatively. "Just because we can't live here doesn't we can't live together."

"What do you mean?"

"I mean not all college students live in expensive beach-front condos. In fact, I don't think any college students live in beach-front condos."

"You mean we could get something in the mountains?"

He laughed. "No. I mean we could get something more modest. Something we could pay for out of our pockets. Something . . . well . . ."

"Cheap?" she whispered.

He nodded.

Lila blinked and backed away. It was such a startling suggestion, she didn't quite know how to respond. Live someplace cheap? Live in a little apartment in town? She couldn't think of anyplace in town that would be suitable. "Bruce," she said. "I've never even seen a doorman building in town."

"We couldn't live in a doorman building even if there were such a thing," he said with a smile. Then he shrugged. "Hey! It was just a crazy idea. Forget it. We'll let this place go and next month, when we get our finances straightened out, we'll try again."

"No!" she cried suddenly, throwing her arms around him. "I want to live with you starting now. I don't care where. Even if we have to live in a hovel, I just want to be with you."

Bruce pulled her closer and pressed his cheek against the top of her head. "You're adorable and that's sweet. But I'm spoiled and you're five times more spoiled than I am. I don't think you could ever be happy in anything less than—"

"As long as I'm with you, I'll be happy," she said, drawing back her head and gazing into his eyes. In them, she saw doubt and hesitation. "Don't you feel the same way?" she asked in a small voice. "I thought you did. I thought it was me you cared about, not the lifestyle."

"Lila! It was my idea to get something cheap that we could afford. But I'm worried that you won't like it."

"I could live in the dirtiest, coldest hole in the world as long as you're in it with me," she insisted.

He put his arms back around her. "Then we'll get our stuff out of here tonight and look for something cheap and cozy tomorrow."

Lila closed her eyes and rested her cheek against Bruce's strong shoulder. Her heart began to thump in pleasant anticipation. It would be romantic to be poor for a while. It would give her a chance to see the real Bruce Patman and him a chance to see the real Lila Fowler. It would give them a chance to fall even more deeply in love.

Chapter Eight

"Listen, Todd. I know all this is really hard for you to take," Elizabeth said. "But no matter what happens, don't lose your temper with Santos today."

"Me? Lose my temper? I'm the mildest-mannered guy in the world."

"C'mon, Todd. This meeting is important. We don't want to blow it. Let Santos do the talking and see what, if anything, we can find out."

"Don't worry. I won't lose my temper, and I'll let you do all the talking," Todd said as they pulled up to the closed wrought-iron gate of the Santos estate. The surrounding fence was overgrown with thick vines and planted with tall trees so that it was impossible to see inside the estate from the drive.

A large man emerged from a brick gatehouse. He wore a suit, not a uniform, but he was obviously some kind of guard. He signaled them to stop.

Todd braked and lowered the window. The

guard leaned down and stared into the car. He didn't smile or speak.

"I'm Todd Wilkins, and this is Elizabeth Wakefield. We're here to see Mr. Santos."

The guard stared at Todd's face another moment.

"We have an appointment," Elizabeth put in.

The man gave them a curt nod. "Wait here." He walked to the gatehouse and picked up a clipboard. His eyes ran down the page, then he picked up a phone mounted on the wall.

"Looks like Mr. Santos is security-conscious," Elizabeth said under her breath.

"I guess it's dangerous work, serving as head of the Alumni Association," Todd joked.

Elizabeth smothered a laugh as the guard returned. He still didn't smile.

"Do you get the idea this guy isn't too thrilled to see us?" Todd whispered.

"Shhh!" Elizabeth warned as the guard bent down to speak.

"Go straight up the drive and park outside the front door of the house," he instructed. "Someone will let you in."

"Thank you," Todd said. "And have a nice day," he added in an ironic tone.

The iron gate swung slowly open, and Todd whistled at the view. Dozens of lushly landscaped acres stretched out before them. It looked like a park.

"Wow! This place is amazing. Look at that." Todd pointed to a man-made pond with five graceful white swans swimming in languid circles in it.

"Look over to your right," Elizabeth said. "Stables."

On the other side of an emerald green field were five immaculate-looking horse barns with red roofs. Beside the barns was a white-fenced ring and inside it, a trainer put two prancing black horses through their paces.

"Those horses are beauties," Todd commented.

"Thoroughbred racehorses," Elizabeth said, her voice full of admiration.

"Horses like that are pretty expensive, aren't they?"

"Expensive doesn't even begin to cover it," Elizabeth said. "Horses like that cost a fortune."

"Everything around here looks like it cost a fortune."

"Don't you think it's strange that you've never been here?" Elizabeth said. "Think of all the alumni parties for the team last fall. Every time I talked to you, you were going out on somebody's boat, or playing golf at somebody's club, or going to a barbecue at somebody's ranch. If you were an alum with money and a place like this, wouldn't you host a major blowout? A party or a picnic?"

Todd nodded. "Yeah, I would. But maybe some people with big money like to keep a low profile," he added darkly.

As they neared the end of the drive they saw the large, rambling, Tudor-style mansion with huge windows and soaring gables.

Todd brought the car to a stop, and they both stepped out. Two large men in suits came hurrying toward them, their wing-tip shoes crunching on the pea gravel. "Mr. Wilkins? Ms. Wakefield?"

Todd nodded.

"Come with us, please."

Elizabeth and Todd exchanged a glance. Neither man had introduced himself. They acted like secret-service agents—barely polite and extremely businesslike.

The enormous, high-ceilinged entrance hall was impressive. The walls were a rich burgundy color, and an oriental runner covered the length of an elaborately inlaid floor.

"This way," the larger of the two men said. He led them down the hall and ushered them into a large paneled den.

A small man in a short-sleeved sport shirt sat behind a desk. He stared at Elizabeth and Todd for a long moment, then his face broke into a friendly smile. "Mr. Wilkins. Ms. Wakefield." He stood and shook their hands. The two men in suits withdrew into the hallway and shut the door.

"Nice of you kids to come by and see me," he said, motioning them over to a sofa and chair. "Sit down. Sit down. I've heard lots of good things about you both. Two very exceptional young people. A credit to Sweet Valley University." He spoke quickly and moved with a darting, energetic gait.

Todd glanced at Elizabeth. Mr. Santos wasn't at all what he was expecting. He wasn't a menacing mobster. And he wasn't a serious business type like Dr. Beal.

91

Mr. Santos was small and balding, with a deep dimple and twinkling eyes. Unlike virtually every other person they had met thus far, he exuded geniality and seemed relaxed.

Elizabeth gave him a charming smile. "That's very nice of you to say, Mr. Santos. We're lucky to be students at SVU. It has a great reputation."

"It does. It does," Mr. Santos agreed cordially. "And a lot of people have worked very hard to make sure that reputation is deserved." He crossed his legs and sat back, lifting his eyebrows inquisitively, as if asking them—in the friendliest way possible—to get to the point.

"How long have you been involved with the Alumni Association, Mr. Santos?" Elizabeth asked with a bland smile, ignoring the hint.

Mr. Santos opened a humidor sitting on the table beside his chair. He examined the cigars inside like a child choosing a piece of candy. He made his selection, then put one in his mouth. "That would be a hard question to answer, Ms. Wakefield." He sat back and lit the cigar with a musing look on his face, then snapped his lighter shut and returned Elizabeth's bland smile. "I was involved for many years before I assumed an"—he hesitated and seemed to be searching for the right word—"official role."

"That's really nice," Elizabeth said. She turned to Todd. "Don't you think it's great when graduates of a university try to give something back to the institution that helped them"—she looked around and gestured in an expansive way to point out his very material success—"become so successful?"

Mr. Santos smiled again and acknowledged the acclaim with a slight bow of his head.

"What year did you graduate?" she asked.

Nothing in Mr. Santos's face changed, but Todd sensed a shift. There was an almost imperceptible tightening of his facial muscles. His genial smile frayed a bit at the edges. In an instant Mr. Santos's relaxed, playful charm transformed into something tense, guarded, and crackling with danger.

Mr. Santos puffed on his cigar a moment, as if carefully considering how to answer the question. Then he uncrossed his legs, leaned forward, and tapped the ash from his cigar into an ashtray on the coffee table. "Ms. Wakefield," he said with a disarming smile. "Some lessons you don't learn in the classroom. Some lessons you learn from life. Live long enough, and you can't help but get an education."

He put down his cigar and opened his hands in imitation of Elizabeth's gesture. "As you say, Ms. Wakefield, my education has helped me to acquire a certain degree of success. And after I made some substantial contributions to Sweet Valley University, they did me the honor of acknowledging my education." He gestured behind him toward a framed diploma.

"So your degree is honorary?" Elizabeth asked in a carefully neutral voice. "You never actually attended the school?"

Mr. Santos shut the top of the humidor with a snap that clearly meant that this part of the conversation was over. "So, tell me, what can I do for you two?" he asked bluntly.

"We're actually here on my behalf," Todd said. "I'm not sure whether you're aware of the circumstances that led to the revocation of my spot on the basketball team, but . . ."

Mr. Santos waved the cigar. "I know about that. Beal . . . I mean Dr. Beal . . . sent me all the files."

Todd drummed his fingers lightly on the arm of the leather chair. "Then I'm sure you know that all my teachers and friends and even my coach have sent letters asking that I be allowed to play again. Dr. Beal, though, said he wasn't prepared to put me back on the team because he felt the Alumni Association might object. I thought if you met me and we had a chance to talk, you might persuade the association to reconsider."

"So what is it you want? You want your scholarship back and you want to play basketball again?"

"That's right."

Mr. Santos stubbed out his cigar. "No problem. I'll send Beal . . . Dr. Beal . . . a letter today."

Todd gave Santos a crooked smile. "You mean it's all settled? Just like that?"

Mr. Santos winked. "Just like that. You came to the right place, kid."

Mr. Santos stood and so did they. He put his arm around Todd's shoulders and gave them a paternal squeeze as he walked him to the door. "There's one thing you could do for me, though, Todd."

"What's that?"

"Stop making so many phone calls," Mr. Santos said softly. "It could be bad for your health."

Todd felt the color drain from his face. "And what if I don't?" he asked evenly.

Mr. Santos smiled genially at them both. "Think about this, Todd. All an athlete really has is his health. You wouldn't want to jeopardize that, would you?"

Todd's temple began to throb, and he shook off Santos's arm. "You know what, Santos . . . Mr. Santos . . . why don't you skip the letter. I'm not going to have time to play basketball. I'll be too busy making phone calls. Come on, Elizabeth."

He grabbed Elizabeth's hand and the two of them stormed out of the den, down the long, dark hall and toward the front door. Santos was a crook and a gambler, Todd thought. He was clearly involved in the point-shaving scam and he was obviously dangerous.

Todd half expected to hear footsteps chasing behind them.

But no armed thugs appeared from any of the rooms to harass them. Outside, they scrambled into the car, and Todd turned on the engine. His hands were shaking with rage.

"Was that a smart thing to do, Todd?" Elizabeth asked through teeth that were slightly gritted.

"I couldn't help it," Todd said, backing out of the drive with the tires squealing. "I don't like what that guy's doing to athletes. They're using fear and exploitation and intimidation to ruin future careers."

"Yeah!" Elizabeth said in a voice of exaggerated patience. "But I think you just made our job a little harder. Now Santos knows what we know. And we don't know any more than we did when we got here."

"Yes, we do. Before we suspected. Now we know," Todd said as they drove out the elaborate front gate. It was all he could do not to run over the flinty-eyed gatekeeper.

Winston's heart pounded in his chest. Professor Stark hadn't said a word yet, but Winston knew exactly why he had asked him to meet him in his office this morning. "Sit down, Winston," he said, leading him into the office with a cup of coffee in his hand.

Professor Stark shut the door, and Winston sat down in one of the straight-backed chairs across from his desk. Professor Stark sat down with his cup of coffee, shuffled through some papers on his desk, located one, and flipped it across the desk toward Winston. "Congratulations," he said in a flat voice. He tilted the cup and took a deep swallow of coffee.

Winston picked up the paper and looked down at it. It was his exam. He'd gotten an A-plus.

He lifted his eyes and looked across the desk at Professor Stark. Neither one of them said anything. Professor Stark took another sip of his coffee, grimaced as if it had produced a stomach pain, and put down the cup. "Mr. Egbert, these conversations are never easy. They degrade both parties. But I am nonetheless forced to ask you this question. Did you cheat on the exam?"

Winston's heart was pounding so loudly, he wondered why Professor Stark wasn't tapping his foot to the beat. His face was red and he felt like he had the flu—hot and cold at the same time. Beads of perspiration formed on his upper lip. He'd been insane. Absolutely insane. He'd let the novelty of knowing the answers go to his head. He should have missed at least two or three to make it look good. Where had his brains been?

With Denise, that's where.

Every minute of every day, Winston thought about Denise. He wondered where she was and what she was doing. He imagined the funny things she was saying and the even funnier things she was thinking.

"Mr. Egbert," Professor Stark repeated. "Did you cheat on this exam?"

"Why do you ask?" Winston couldn't help responding, even though he knew it was the stupidest question in the world. And the fact that his voice sounded like air leaking out of a balloon pegged him as guilty with a capital *G*.

"I ask for two reasons," Professor Stark answered softly. "One. You have shown no previous aptitude for this subject matter. In fact, you were so uncertain of your ability to learn the material in time for the exam that you begged me for some extra credit. I was unable to accommodate you in that regard, but I did prepare some study sheets for you. Which brings me to reason number two. You never picked up those study sheets."

"I didn't?" Winston squeaked.

"I found them crumpled into a ball on my desk that afternoon when I came in." He held up an envelope for Winston that had his name scrawled across the front. "I left this on my desk for you and asked Professor Miles to give it to you in my absence."

"Oh, I guess I forgot to take it with me."

Professor Stark frowned. "Forgot to take it with you? When?"

Winston paled. "When I, uh . . . When I . . ."

"Were you here in this office?"

Winston hung his head. "Yes."

"How did you get in? Professor Miles said he didn't see you."

"Professor Miles had given Jessica Wakefield the key," Winston explained softly. "I came in with her, and while she was waiting for Professor Miles, I . . ." Winston pushed his hair back off his forehead. "I saw the tests on your desk and I took one."

"I see." Professor Stark held out his hand, and Winston gave him back the test.

"You will receive an F, of course," Professor Stark said in a voice that took no pleasure in the announcement. He lifted his hands and rubbed his forehead, as if he felt ill.

"Will I be expelled?" Winston asked fearfully.

"I honestly don't know, Mr. Egbert. The administration must be informed. Your parents will be called and asked to come for a conference. A decision will be made at that time."

"Oh," Winston said weakly.

Professor Stark removed his glasses, pinched the bridge of his nose, and laid them deliberately down on the desk. He took a sip of his coffee and sat back in his chair with the air of a man who had received a terrible blow. "Mr. Egbert, I think you're a very well intentioned young man who means no harm."

Winston nodded. "I am. And I don't."

"If you're expelled, you will probably spend the rest of your life feeling that you were unfairly punished for a trivial offense."

Winston said nothing, but Stark was right. Winston was sorry. But in the big scheme of things, it was just one physics test. And it wasn't as if he was going to actually be a physicist or anything like that.

"I think you should understand why cheating cannot and should not be tolerated," Professor Stark continued. "It is said that when you cheat, you cheat only yourself. Like most platitudes, it is not true, Mr. Egbert." Professor Stark's voice was nonjudgmental, but he was obviously very serious about what he was saying. "Cheaters erode the academic credibility of a university. When you cheated, you cheated every single student who attends this university and expects their diploma to be respected in the job market. College educations are expensive. They are a major investment. Some people work their whole lives in order to pay for one. When you devalue your fellow students' diplomas, you quite literally rob them of their investment. As a member of the faculty, my value, my salary, is a function of the degree to which this university is respected. If it is not respected, I am not respected. And Mr. Egbert, I deserve to be respected. I am a PhD in physics. I worked very hard to acquire my body of knowledge. And I cannot help but resent someone who seeks to trivialize what I have achieved."

Winston looked at Professor Stark. He was stuffy, but he was a nice guy. And he was talking very sincerely. Not yelling. Not sermonizing. Just laying it on the line and letting Winston know that he took his work very seriously, and he took cheating very personally.

"Is there anything I can do to . . ." Winston cast about for the appropriate words. *Make it up to you* wasn't quite right. But he wanted Stark to know that he hadn't meant to insult him.

Professor Stark shook his head sadly.

"I'm sorry," Winston said softly.

"So am I," Professor Stark responded, reaching for the telephone.

Chapter
Nine

"What are you still doing here?" Elizabeth came hurrying into the room and threw her backpack and jacket on the bed.

Jessica looked guiltily up from her nest of pillows and blankets. "I live here, remember?" She laughed weakly, trying to smile as if there were nothing unusual about the fact that it was almost time for lunch and she was still in bed.

Elizabeth frowned. "Are you sick?"

"No."

"Then why aren't you up and dressed?"

Because I'm so afraid of missing his call, I can't even get into the shower.

But of course, she couldn't tell Elizabeth that. She couldn't tell Elizabeth that she had skipped her morning classes, breakfast, coffee—everything—because she was waiting for a phone call. *Ring*, she mentally willed the phone. *Please ring.*

Jessica's mind worked feverishly, trying to come up with some kind of explanation. "I'm too tired to go to class. I'm worn out from helping Bruce and Lila move into their condo," she said as Elizabeth went over to the closet and began rifling through it.

Her sister shook her head. "I give it exactly twenty-four hours."

"What do you mean?" Jessica asked.

Elizabeth removed her thin red cashmere sweater and changed into a cotton blouse. "It's getting hot out there," she muttered absently. She went to the window and opened it wider, looking thoughtfully out over the campus.

"What do you mean, you give it twenty-four hours?" Jessica repeated.

"What I mean is that I don't think Bruce and Lila are going to last very long playing house," she answered in an abstracted voice, as if it didn't matter much to her one way or the other.

"But they're in love."

Elizabeth took some deep breaths while she thought it over, then chuckled. "Maybe. Maybe not. I guess this way they'll find out for sure."

Suddenly Jessica was furious. She sat up. "Why are you always so smug about stuff like this?" she demanded. "You and Tom are in love and you say it's serious. But you always act like other people's relationships are just superficial crushes. Do you think you're the only person on this campus capable of falling in love for real?"

Elizabeth gave Jessica an amazed look.

Jessica knew she'd probably overreacted, but she didn't feel like apologizing. "Excuse me." She threw off her covers, jumped out of bed, and ran out into the hall toward the bathroom.

Jessica hurried into a stall, closed the door behind her, and locked it. Hot tears began to trickle down her cheeks, and she rested her head against the metal door. Why hadn't he called? Why?

She'd lain awake practically all night, waiting for Louis to call. He'd said he'd call. He'd promised he'd call.

Jessica wished she could bang her head on the door hard enough to drive away all the pictures in her mind that were torturing her. All night she had seen the same image—Louis raking away a tangle of dark curls on that other woman's head.

Why am I putting myself through all this? she wondered miserably. This was exactly the way she had decided not to feel anymore.

"Jess!" Elizabeth called from the other side of the door. "I'm sorry if I said something wrong. Please come out."

Jessica ignored her sister's voice. She heard the faint sound of a phone ringing down the hall.

"There's the phone," Elizabeth said. "I'll get it."

But Jessica flew out of the bathroom stall so fast she practically knocked Elizabeth over. "Relax," she heard Elizabeth yell as she raced down the hall. "I turned on the machine."

The door to their room was open, and Jessica

103

ran in and threw herself at the phone. "Hello?" she answered breathlessly, almost yanking the phone out of the wall.

There was no answer.

"Hello?" she said again, holding her breath so that her own breathing didn't interfere with her ability to hear.

Elizabeth appeared in the doorway, shaking her head at Jessica's antics.

"Hello?" Was that breathing on the other end of the line or just dead air? "Is anybody there?" she asked in mounting frustration. "Louis?"

There was a soft click. Whoever had called replaced the receiver without saying a word.

Disappointed, Jessica hung up. She turned and saw Elizabeth staring at her with her hands on her hips. "Who is Louis?" Elizabeth asked with a sympathetic smile.

Jessica caught her breath, then exhaled. Elizabeth would know who "Professor Miles" was. Everybody on campus knew who he was. There weren't many new professors. And there weren't any whose good looks had been as talked about and admired. But there was no way Elizabeth could know who "Louis" was.

"He's a guy in biology class," Jessica lied.

"Aha. Now I'm beginning to get the picture. You've got a new guy. His name is Louis. This time, it's the real thing," Elizabeth teased lightly. "True love. Right?"

"Shut up," Jessica begged. "Please. He's just a

guy who said he'd take notes for me this morning," she lied. "Don't make a big deal out of it. I told you before, I'm through with love." Jessica trudged back into the bathroom and splashed some water on her face.

Elizabeth followed her in. "Jess," she said in a conciliatory tone. "I'm sorry. I didn't mean to make fun of Bruce and Lila. And I know you've been going through a rough time. Is there anything I can do?"

Jessica pressed the cold, wet cloth against her face. "No. But thanks."

"Want to talk about it?"

Jessica shook her head. "No." She lifted her head and saw Elizabeth gazing quizzically at her in the mirror. She forced a smile. "And you're right. I do have another silly crush, but it's not anybody in my biology class and it's probably not serious."

"Somebody on the football team again?" Elizabeth asked.

"No," Jessica improvised. "He's more . . . uh . . ."

"The fraternity type?"

Jessica didn't want to get caught in a web of complicated lies. So she just winked and gave Elizabeth an enigmatic smile before burying her face in her thick white washcloth. *Ring,* she willed again. *Please, please, please ring.*

"Why are you stopping here?" Lila asked. "I thought we were going back to look at the apartment we saw before. The one across from the beach condo."

"I called this morning and that place was rented," Bruce explained. He pointed toward the FOR RENT sign on the door of a dilapidated three-story Victorian house with a sagging front porch. "But there's a place available in there."

Lila's head snapped in his direction with her mouth open. "You're not serious," she finally said when she had time to catch her breath. "That looks even worse than the first place we saw." Bruce reached behind to the backseat of his Porsche and grabbed a folded piece of newspaper. "According to this ad in the real-estate section, there's a one-bedroom, one-bathroom apartment in there with an efficiency kitchen."

"It looks horrible," Lila protested, arrogantly adjusting the shoulder of her red leather jacket.

Bruce reached over and brushed his finger against her cheek. "Lila, I'm sorry, but right now we can't afford anything better. I don't like it either, but I love you and I want us to live together. I'm willing to go in there and take a look if you are."

Lila faced forward, crossed her arms, and gazed stubbornly out the windshield. Bruce held his breath. He knew Lila cared about him. But when it came down to choosing between him and her own comfort, he had a hard time believing she'd really choose him.

"It's okay," he said, tossing the paper back

into the backseat. "We'll hold off and—"

Lila reached up and grabbed his hand. "No," she said. "Let's go in and take a look." She leaned over and kissed him. Then she quickly hopped out of the car.

Bruce got out and walked around to the sidewalk, taking note of the broken concrete curb and the missing slats in the fence.

"A couple of guys from the fraternity lived in this building last semester," Bruce said in what he hoped was a cheerful voice. They climbed the stairs to the front door and rang. "And they lived to tell about it."

An old lady in a faded housedress and a hairnet opened the door and gazed at them suspiciously. A cigarette dangled from her lips. "Yes?"

"We're here about the apartment," Bruce said.

She squinted at them through her cigarette smoke, as if trying to decide whether they were legitimate apartment hunters or wandering serial killers.

Bruce widened his smile and gave her the Bruce Patman All-American-Boy-Hunk smile. "I'm Bruce Patman, and this is Lila Fowler. Maybe we could take a look?"

She didn't exactly melt, but she did step back, silently inviting them into the front hall.

Bruce saw Lila's nose wrinkle. He didn't blame her. The place had fifty years of cigarette smoke and greasy cooking imbedded in the walls. And the Turkish carpet was so old and faded that the

107

pattern was indistinguishable from the stains.

"I'm Mrs. Finch—the owner and manager. Follow me. I'll show you the apartment." She removed a large bundle of keys from her pocket and began lumbering up the steps. Bruce and Lila climbed behind her.

On the landing of the third floor, Mrs. Finch opened a door and started up yet another set of stairs.

"The apartment's in the attic?" Lila asked.

Mrs. Finch didn't even bother to answer, and Bruce nudged Lila onward. At the top of the stairs, Mrs. Finch opened another door.

Bruce had been prepared for something shabby. But this apartment surpassed his worst nightmares.

The door to the apartment opened right into the living room. There was no front hall. The window that faced the street was hung with a limp yellow curtain full of moth holes. The sofa and chairs looked as if they had been bought fifth hand—or maybe even scavenged from the street.

They crossed the room, entering a narrow hallway barely big enough for two people, never mind three. He looked to his left, over Lila's shoulder, into a tiny bedroom with a slanted ceiling. It was so small, there was room for only one piece of furniture—a sagging bed pushed against the wall.

Bruce turned his horrified gaze across the hall and was confronted by the ugly efficiency kitchen. Rust and grease were caked on the burners of the oven. The linoleum floor was scratched, and there were fingerprints all over the ancient wooden cabinets and refrigerator door.

The bathroom was right next to the kitchen. The door was closed, and Bruce was thankful. If the bathroom was anything like the rest of the place, it was probably unfit for human habitation.

His heart sank. This was no place for Lila. She'd never lived in anything less than luxury accommodations her whole life. She was too spoiled and pampered to ever be happy in a place like this. "Mrs. Finch," Bruce began, shaking his head in apology. "This place is . . ." He broke off when he felt Lila grasp his arm.

"This place is just beautiful," Lila said, smiling mistily at him. "We'll take it."

Chapter Ten

Louis's hand hovered indecisively over the dialing pad. Stark had gone to the administration building. One of his students had cheated, and that always created a big stir. Louis hoped it would keep him out of the office for at least an hour.

If he was going to call, now was the time to do it. He'd delayed too long already. He picked up the phone and then dropped it guiltily when someone tapped softly on his office door. Louis hung up the phone, flustered. "Come in," he invited, expecting some timid student to appear with an essay grade to dispute.

No one answered.

"Hello?" he called out. "Is someone there?"

When there was no response, he tensed, moving quietly and cautiously toward the door. He listened intently for a moment and heard nothing. Perhaps someone had simply knocked on the wrong door.

He smiled. Or perhaps Alison Quinn had decided to stop by and flirt, but changed her mind. It was the kind of thing that went with the territory, and he should be flattered rather than annoyed. Making up his mind to be patient and kind, he opened the door.

His stomach lurched. The hall was deserted. There was no one in sight in either direction. But the smell of heavy rose perfume hung in the air like a black cloud.

Louis backed up and closed the door, locking it behind him. He moved straight for the phone. That smell, that stink, he thought savagely, had just reminded him that he had no choice.

He punched in the numbers, and his heart felt a painful stab when Jessica answered it before the first ring had completed. It meant she'd been waiting for his call. He was important to her now.

Too important.

Why hadn't he kept his feelings to himself? Now there was no way to keep her safe without hurting her. "Jessica, it's Louis."

"Hi."

There was a long pause, and Louis took a deep breath before launching into the speech he'd prepared and rehearsed in his mind. "Jessica. I'm sorry I didn't call you sooner, but I needed a little time to think things over. I've decided that we're both acting like idiots."

He heard her gasp at the other end of the line, but he forced himself to plow ahead. "You're a beautiful woman. And smart and sweet and brave, but what we're doing makes no sense at all. It's too risky to continue. Too dangerous. I don't think we should see each other again."

He closed his eyes and waited for her to respond, steeling himself against a barrage of tears, recriminations, and abuse.

But there were no insults and no accusations. All he heard was Jessica trying to catch her breath at the other end of the line. Every gasp caused a sharp ache in his heart that was so intense, he could hardly keep from gasping himself. Having to hurt the woman he loved was worse than being tortured.

"Why?" It was hardly more than a whisper, and so choked with emotion that he felt a lump rise in his own throat.

Louis swallowed hard, trying to keep his voice steady. "We've been over and over this. I'm a professor. It could damage my career if anyone found out that I was involved with a student."

"I'll drop out of school. I won't be a student. Then there's no problem."

"No!" he responded curtly.

"Louis," she sobbed. "I'd never do anything to cause you trouble. Never. I'd give my life for you. But there's got to be some way to work this out."

"I don't want to discuss it," he snapped.

"How can we work this out if you won't even discuss it? I don't understand why you're acting like this. You said . . ."

"Jessica," he said, forcing his voice to sound cold

and matter-of-fact. "From the very beginning, my fear was that you weren't mature enough for me. This conversation is convincing me that I was right. I don't think we should have any further contact between us. After you've had a chance to think it over, you'll arrive at the same conclusion. Good-bye, Jessica."

He hung up the phone as if letting go of a snake, then he put his head down on his desk and began to cry. Tears of regret, pain, and grief soaked into the fabric of his tweed jacket.

"I would give my life for you," Jessica had said.

She didn't know how very real a possibility that was. But he wasn't going to let her find out.

Lila arranged the vegetables on the roasting pan, humming to herself. So far, she was having a ball. She and Bruce had spent most of the day moving in their stuff. After that, they'd gone to the grocery store just like a real married couple.

Since neither one of them knew anything about cooking, they'd decided to roast a pan of vegetables. How hard could that be? Wash them. Peel them. Put them in a pan and shove them in the oven.

"Lila," Bruce called from the living room. "I'm going down to get the stereo out of the trunk. How are you doing in there?"

"Okay, except for the fact that everything's covered with grime."

"I'll get some steel wool tomorrow and see what I can do. Be back in a minute." She heard the door close as he left.

Lila sighed dreamily. It was all so domestic. She hummed a little louder as she rearranged the yellow squash and red pepper so that they were more attractively positioned. Using the tips of her fingers, she turned the greasy knob to "bake" and placed the pan in the oven.

There were a few peelings left on the counter, and she picked them up and put them in the paper sack they were using for a garbage can. She washed her hands with some dish-washing liquid. They'd forgotten to get paper towels, so she went into the bathroom and used one of her bath towels.

While she was in the bathroom, she freshened her lipstick and fluffed her hair a little.

"Honey! I'm home," Bruce called out from the living room.

Lila giggled and walked out of the bathroom with the towel over her shoulder. "Dinner in five minutes, dear." She walked into the tiny kitchen and opened the oven door to check the progress of the vegetables. "Bruce. I don't think this oven's working. It's not hot."

Bruce came in the kitchen and peered into the oven over her shoulder. "It's a gas oven," he said. "You have to light the pilot." He grabbed a box of kitchen matches from the counter. "Let me get where you are." Lila backed up so Bruce could get to the oven. She stood behind him so she could watch what he was doing.

He opened the box, struck the match, and . . .

"Yeow!" he yelled.

Lila shrieked as the blast from the oven sent Bruce reeling backward with his bangs on fire. She threw the towel over his head, smothering the flames as they both stumbled out of the kitchen.

Bruce pulled the towel from his head and gulped. When he had his breath, he lurched back into the kitchen and turned off the gas. "How long had that thing been on?"

Lila shrugged. "I don't know. Five minutes, maybe."

"Five minutes! That thing's been spitting out gas for five minutes! Why didn't you tell me? It's a wonder we didn't blow the whole place sky-high."

"How was I supposed to know? At my house, the maid just turns on the oven and that's all there is to it."

Bruce gaped at her. "That's because you have an electric oven."

"So?"

He threw up his arms, and his eyes bulged like he was talking to the stupidest person in the whole world. "Don't you know the difference between a gas oven and an electric oven?" he yelled.

"No, I don't," she yelled back. "And you know what? I don't care. I've never cooked anything before in my whole life, and I'm never cooking anything again." Lila marched into the bathroom and shut the door with a bang.

Bruce knocked at the door. "Lila. Let me in. I need to get to the medicine cabinet."

"We don't have one," she reminded him scornfully. She glanced resentfully at the exposed-glass shelves above the toilet where their various cosmetics and hair products were stacked.

"I need some ointment or something."

"Go to the drugstore."

"Come on, Lila!" Bruce begged in an exasperated voice. "I've got third-degree burns out here and you're giving me a hard time. What kind of person are you?"

She went to the door and kicked it. "The kind of person who doesn't know the difference between a gas oven and an electric oven?"

"Lila! Come out," he ordered in an aggressive tone.

She drew herself up. Where did he get off giving her orders? Who did he think he was? "Forget it."

He banged violently on the door. "Come out of there right now or I'll break the door down."

"Are you crazy?"

"No. The kitchen is on fire!" he shouted. "Get out of there."

Lila unlocked the door and jerked it open in time to see Bruce running into the kitchen, where black smoke poured through the door. "Bruce. No! Come back!"

"Call the fire department," he yelled.

Lila raced to the telephone, but when she picked it up, there was no dial tone. The phone was dead.

116

Chapter Eleven

Winston trudged toward his dorm, Oakley Hall, feeling like a man under indictment for murder. But his heart lightened a little when he saw Denise standing in the doorway.

She was dressed in one of his vintage bowling shirts tucked into a pair of baggy men's pants cinched at her tiny waist. "Winston!" She ran out to meet him and threw her arms around him. "Where have you been? I've been waiting around the dorm for you all day."

Winston had been out walking. All over. Uptown. Downtown. Across town.

Meandering through stores. Wandering into coffee shops. Studying menus and walking out because eating was impossible. Even if he could get food past his throat—which felt like he had nine rubber bands around it—his stomach was so queasy he wouldn't be able to keep anything down.

"I've missed you." She kissed his cheek and forehead. "And I was just about to get mad. Did you forget about me?"

Winston kissed her back. It felt good to have Denise in his arms again. He'd told her he needed some time to study, and she'd agreed to give him a little space. But she had made him promise they'd get together as soon as his exam was over and he'd had a chance to recuperate from his all-nighter. "I could never forget about you," he said sincerely.

"There's a Marx Brothers film festival at the Multiplex," Denise chattered happily. "If we hurry, we can make the second feature."

"Um, not tonight," he said softly.

Denise backed up and studied him. "What's wrong!" she asked, her face registering alarm. "You look awful. Are you sick? What hurts?"

"Let's go inside," he said, taking her by the hand. "We need to talk. In private."

"Sure," Denise answered in a concerned voice. "Come on." She gave his hand a comforting squeeze and walked with him in silence to his door. He tried to put his key into the lock, but his hand was shaking too badly.

Denise gasped and took the key from his hand. "Let's go to the health center," she said decisively. "You are sick."

He shook his head. "No, I'm not sick. I'm just scared. Open the door for me, *please*," he instructed.

Quickly Denise opened the door and helped him inside. Winston closed it firmly and locked it, as if he could barricade himself against his impending doom. "I've got to tell you something," he said, beginning to calm down now that he was in the safety of his own room with the woman he loved. "I think you'd better sit."

Denise's knees buckled. "Somebody died?" She collapsed on the edge of the bed. "Who? Somebody I know? One of our friends?"

Winston lifted his hands. "Nobody died."

Her eyelids fluttered slowly shut in relief, then popped open. "Then what could possibly be so awful that it's making your face look so green?"

He sat down beside her and took her hand in his. "I cheated on a test and I got caught."

"What!"

"I cheated on the physics exam. I got caught. The school called my parents. They're coming here tomorrow. I'm probably going to be expelled."

Her eyes grew large and confused. "I still don't understand. What do you mean, you cheated?"

"I mean, I cheated," Winston said. "I stole a copy of the test from Professor Stark's office and looked up all the answers to the questions in advance."

"This is insane," she protested. "I can't believe what I'm hearing. You're making it up."

"No. I'm not."

"Is this a joke?"

"No," Winston repeated slowly. "I wish it were."

"But you're not a cheater," Denise insisted. "You're not the type. You're one of the most honest people I know. Why would you do something like that?"

"My physics grade was low. I was afraid if I didn't do well, my parents would pressure me to change schools."

Denise's face began to harden. She slowly withdrew her hand from his. "You cheated," she whispered. "You deliberately cheated. You actually planned it. You had time to think about it, and then you did it."

"Denise, please believe me—I've never done it before and I'll never do it again."

"I guess not," she said dryly. "The consequences are pretty unpleasant. But frankly, Winston, I would respect someone who doesn't cheat because they're honest, not just because they're afraid of getting caught."

"It's not like that. Really, Denise. You've got it wrong. I'm sorry I did it—not just because I got caught but because . . . because . . ." He trailed off, sputtering. His mind was spinning in confusion. He tried to reconstruct what Stark had said to him. But it was so complicated and convoluted, and he was so upset. He couldn't even begin to clearly articulate what he had learned from the experience.

Denise was backing away from him, and

Winston felt so awful he wanted to scream with anguish. He wanted to clutch at the leg of her pants and beg her not to go. "Please don't leave me," he whispered. "Please, Denise. Don't leave me."

Her cheeks were wet with tears. "You cheated," she choked. She looked as ill as Winston felt. "You're not the person I thought you were."

"I had a good reason!" he wailed, tears running down his cheeks.

Her lips were trembling and she shook her head as if she had taken a blow.

"I did it for you!" he cried, stretching his long arms toward her.

"What?" she gasped.

"I did it for you. Because I love you."

"For me?" she yelled through her tears. "What does that mean?"

"I was afraid that if I didn't pass the test and my parents made me change schools, we wouldn't be together anymore. I did it for you. Don't you see? I did it because I love you."

Denise's face turned red with fury. She marched toward him, lifted her hand, and struck him across the face. "Don't ever speak to me again," she said. "You're a cheater. And a whiner. Don't you ever blame me for your mistakes. Be a man, Winston. For once in your life be a man." She ran to the door, fumbled with the lock, and then stormed out, slamming it shut behind her.

Winston fell face forward onto his pillow and began to weep.

Late that night, Lila sat down on the couch and laid her head in the cradle of Bruce's shoulder. "I can't believe it."

Bruce stretched his legs out alongside hers. "What a day," he said with a laugh. "We found an apartment. Moved our stuff. Practically blew ourselves up with the oven, and nearly suffocated. How could a piece of burning yellow squash create that much smoke?"

Lila began to laugh too. "I've always known that being poor was unpleasant. But nobody told me how dangerous it was."

She felt Bruce's chest rise and fall as he chuckled. "Thank goodness the telephone didn't work. Can you imagine how embarrassing it would have been to have the fire department come running over here to hose down some overcooked vegetables?"

"I think we should plan on summering in Paris. We could take some cooking classes at the Cordon Bleu."

"In the meantime I think we'd better plan on eating a lot of takeout. And you'd better give me a lot of attention. I think I'm permanently traumatized."

Lila lifted her head, looked at his singed eyebrows and bangs, and giggled again. "Poor baby."

"Ha ha, yourself," he said dryly. "You almost killed me, you know."

"You rallied enough to go out for pizza."

"That's because I'm the stoic, uncomplaining type."

"No, you're not. You were just hungry."

Bruce smiled. The telephone hadn't worked because the previous tenant had left without paying his bill. So after clearing some of the smoke out of the apartment, Bruce had rubbed a little ointment on his singed brows and gone out to pick up a pizza.

Unfortunately on the way home, he'd gotten caught in a thunderstorm. By the time he arrived back at the apartment, both he and the pizza were drenched.

Still, Lila had managed to find a candle and some matches, and the two of them had shared a romantic candlelight dinner for two. A dinner consisting of wet, doughy pizza and tap water.

Now, in the after-dinner quiet, Lila lay against Bruce's chest and felt content. She closed her eyes and let her imagination run wild. Maybe, with a little luck, her father and his lawyers would get her affairs untangled soon. If she could spend a little money on this place, she could turn it into the coziest, most romantic apartment in California.

She sighed dreamily, imagining the shabby, dusty old furniture replaced with some overstuffed Victorian pieces. She'd put turn-of-the-century upholstery and tassels on everything.

A Chinese screen in the corner would hide the ugly heating unit. But first, that naked bulb that hung from the ceiling had to go. She'd replace it with a small, glittering crystal-and-gilt chandelier.

She felt Bruce's finger stroke the line of her ear. "Thinking about me?" he asked in a low, romantic voice.

"Actually, I was mentally redecorating," she murmured.

"Don't get too carried away," he said. "If Uncle Dan is dead set against this, he can just re-invest the dividends next month and keep me on a short string indefinitely."

Lila sat up and frowned. "You're kidding."

He gave her an apologetic smile. "I wish I were."

"Why didn't you tell me?"

"I didn't think of it until just now. While you were mentally redecorating, I was mentally review-ing my trust agreement. If he wants to keep my money from me, he can."

"This is awful!" Lila wailed.

"I thought you didn't care where we lived as long as we were together."

Lila saw the hurt on his face and immediately felt terrible. She realized this whole situation was making him feel very inadequate. But it wasn't his fault.

Well, actually, it was his fault.

But it didn't matter. She loved him anyway. "You're right. I don't care where we live. As long as I'm with you, I'm happy."

They stared into each other's eyes for a long moment. The candle on the floor began to sputter out just as the rain began again, beating softly on the roof above them. Lila caught a last, golden glimpse of Bruce's profile before the candle was completely extinguished. "Oh, Bruce," she whispered, brushing her lips against his.

"Lila!" he murmured, his voice thick with emotion.

She felt his arms tighten around her shoulders and pull her closer when suddenly, something whacked her on the head. The next thing she knew, somebody dumped a bucket of water on them.

"What the—!" they both screamed, jumping up from the sofa.

Bruce dove for the light and they both looked around in a panic. They looked left.

Nothing.

They looked right.

Nothing.

They stared at each other in horror, then slowly turned their eyes upward. A huge chunk of plaster had fallen out of the ceiling, and water from the roof was pouring down into their apartment.

"Jessica?" Elizabeth whispered, quietly entering the room. "Are you awake?"

Jessica lay facedown on her pillow and didn't answer. She didn't want Elizabeth to see her swollen eyes and start asking a lot of questions. She couldn't stand to talk about it. Not yet.

Even if she were willing to, she probably couldn't. She felt sure that if she tried to talk, she would have no voice.

After crying for hours, her head was throbbing and her throat felt raw and dry. Her whole body felt wrung out—like there wasn't a tear left anywhere in her. She blinked. There was a scratchy, sandy feeling behind her lids.

Elizabeth softly tiptoed around the room, trying not to wake her. She turned on the low light beside her bed with a soft snap and began quietly undressing on her side of the room.

The pillow beneath Jessica's cheek was soaking wet and it made the fabric of the pillowcase feel coarse and irritating against her skin.

As soon as Elizabeth left the room, Jessica flipped her pillow and rolled over on her back. "Oh, Louis," she whispered in the dark. "Why didn't you just leave me alone? Why did you make me fall in love with you? I can't bear this."

Miserably she turned to face the wall again. Her entire body throbbed with a dull ache. Her knees. Her jaw. The joints of her wrists and hands.

But it wasn't a good kind of ache—the kind of ache she felt after a hard workout, the kind that reminded her she was young, healthy, and alive.

No. This was the bad kind of hurt. It was the searing burn of longing, regret, humiliation, and disappointment.

Jessica's breath was slow and measured, and it felt as if her heart began to beat slower and slower. Maybe a person really could die from a broken heart. If so, she was knocking on death's door.

Chapter Twelve

Elizabeth pulled a green sweater on over her khakis and picked up her hairbrush. With a few swift strokes, she gathered her long blond hair into a ponytail that she could pull through the back of her SVU baseball cap.

She was exhausted after spending most of the night at the computer. Gin-Yung had given her massive amounts of data, and she was almost finished with the inputting. What she wanted now was some coffee and a quick breakfast. Then she'd hit the computer again. Another two hours and she'd be ready to analyze the information.

The phone rang as she was adjusting the cap. She glanced over at Jessica's bed. Her sister didn't stir. Elizabeth picked up the receiver and turned her back to keep the noise level as low as possible. "Hello?" she said softly.

"I just heard from Mark," Todd's voice said at the other end of the line.

"What did he say? Where has he been?"

"He said he's been thinking things over. But he wants to talk to us."

"Where and when?"

"He called from town. So I said we'd meet him at the corner of Holcombe and Briar in fifteen minutes. That okay with you?"

Elizabeth felt a surge of adrenaline. All they needed to prove their story was one person willing to talk. Maybe it would be Mark. "That's fine with me," she said eagerly.

"I'll pick you up in five minutes," Todd said.

"I'll be ready," Elizabeth answered. She hung up the phone and turned around. Jessica's eyes were open, but she lay perfectly still and showed no sign that she was planning to get up. Elizabeth put her hands on her hips. "Are you going to get out of bed and dressed today?"

"No," Jessica said flatly.

"Why not?"

"I don't feel like it."

"If you don't get up, I'm going to call the doctor. I mean it."

Jessica curled into a ball and pulled her quilt up to her chin. "I don't want a doctor," she muttered listlessly. "I'm not sick. Leave me alone."

"You look sick."

"I'm just sick of school."

Elizabeth watched Jessica and tried to decide

128

how worried to be. Jessica was impulsive, emotional, and self-indulgent. But she wasn't lazy. At least not physically.

Her sister was perfectly capable of goofing off for days at a time. She could spend hours hanging around the room reading magazines, doing her nails, and talking on the telephone with her girlfriends. But it was unusual for her to stay in bed unless she was sick.

Still, it was even more unusual for Jessica to suffer in silence. When Jessica didn't feel well, she didn't hesitate to complain.

Elizabeth ran a mental review of the last few weeks. There had been a two-week period during which Jessica had gone out almost every night with Randy Mason and stayed out late. Maybe that marathon was finally catching up with her. If so, it was sure taking its toll. Not even Jessica's new secret crush was enough to get her up and out of bed.

"You've got class in half an hour," Elizabeth scolded. "And you missed all your classes yesterday." She reached down, grabbed the quilt, and pulled it off. "Get up! Because if you flunk out, you'll have to go home. I don't want to have to get used to a new roommate at this point in the year."

Jessica groaned and rolled out of bed sideways, putting her feet on the floor and reluctantly sitting up. Elizabeth sat down beside her and rubbed her shoulders like a fight coach. "Atta girl," she teased in mock-macho encouragement. "Up and at 'em. You got places to go and people to see." *And so do*

129

I, she thought with a flicker of excitement.

Jessica yawned and stood. "Okay, okay. I'm awake. I'm up." Elizabeth watched her grab a terry-cloth robe and bath kit and stumble toward the door on her way to the bathroom. She looked at her watch. Did she have time to run out and get Jessica a cup of coffee? Unfortunately, no. Todd would be here to pick her up any minute.

She grabbed her bag and left the room. On the way down the hall, Elizabeth stopped in the bathroom. She knocked on the door of the only occupied shower stall. "I'm leaving, Jessica. Promise me you won't go back to bed as soon as I disappear," she shouted over the noise of the water.

There was no answer.

"Jessica!" Elizabeth prompted in an ominous tone.

"All right," Jessica grudgingly agreed from the other side of the door.

Her voice sounded more awake, and Elizabeth felt encouraged. Once Jessica had a shower and got dressed, she'd feel more like her old self. "What's your first class? In case I want to check on you," Elizabeth joked.

There was no answer.

"Jess?" Elizabeth pressed. "What's your first class?"

"Medieval History."

The minute she heard Elizabeth leave, Jessica got out of the shower, pulled on her robe, and padded down the hall toward their room, wondering what to wear.

As hurt and anguished as she felt, she wanted to see Louis. She needed to see him.

Almost hating herself for being so weak, she decided to wear the same outfit she had worn the day he'd kissed her on the beach. The outfit made her look great, and she needed all the confidence she could muster. Besides that, if he saw her looking the way she had that day, maybe he would change his mind about their relationship.

If she could talk to him, maybe she could convince him that she was as concerned about his job as he was. Maybe he thought she wasn't capable of keeping a secret?

If he thought she was a gossiping sorority girl like Alison and some of the other Thetas he'd met at breakfast, no wonder he thought the risk was too great. She pulled the sweater on over her head with a renewed sense of hope.

Mark looked at his watch. He was late. In the last ten minutes, he had changed his mind four times about meeting Todd and Elizabeth. Being near the campus brought back painful memories and lots and lots of anger.

He remembered the unfriendly looks he'd encountered in the cafeteria. Why had he let Wilkins talk him into giving SVU another chance to reject him and put him down? He was just about to turn on his heel when he spotted

Wilkins and Elizabeth across the street.

"Mark!" Todd cried, waving his hand in a friendly greeting. Todd looked quickly both ways for traffic and ran across the street to meet him. Todd looked so genuinely glad to see him that Mark momentarily forgot his anger and accepted Todd's warm hug. "Good to see you, man."

"Good to see you too, Wilkins." He nodded at Elizabeth, and she nodded back. She didn't look unfriendly, but she looked like she didn't care too much for Mark Gathers.

"So what's this all about?" Mark asked, pushing the uncomfortable subject of Alex to the back of his mind.

"Come on," Todd said, leading the way. "There's a little bakery down the street with an outdoor café in back. It's usually pretty empty this time of day."

Mark followed Todd and Elizabeth into the bakery. Todd went to the counter to get their coffee, and Mark and Elizabeth walked through the fresh-smelling shop and out the back door to the little patio. There were several tables, but none were occupied.

"How about here?" Elizabeth suggested, pointing to a little table in the sun.

"So how have you been?" Mark asked her as they took their seats and waited for Todd to come with the coffee. "I read about that William White thing in the paper. Must have been a pretty hairy experience having an insane stalker try to murder you and all your friends."

132

Elizabeth settled back into her chair and gave him a level stare. "It was. You can't imagine how horrible it was. For me. And for Todd. We were threatened, intimidated, and harassed." She gave Mark a significant look. "I don't like being treated that way. And neither does Todd. We didn't take it lying down."

Todd appeared with three cups of coffee. He put them down and dropped a fistful of sugar packets and stirrers in the center of the table. "What did I miss?"

"I was just telling Mark that when William White tried to ruin our lives, we didn't take it lying down."

There was so much cryptic antagonism in her voice, Mark felt himself bristle. "If you're trying to tell me something, Elizabeth, spit it out." He looked at Todd. "Let's skip the bull and cut to the chase. What do you want?"

Todd took a sip of his coffee. "I asked you before, when we talked on the phone, if anybody ever offered you money to play for SVU."

"I told you no then. And the answer is still no."

"Then how do you explain the car?" Elizabeth asked, her voice tinged with suspicion.

"What's to explain?"

"You're driving a pretty expensive car for somebody in college."

"I got a good price and a low-interest loan," Mark said, working hard to keep his temper in check.

"Based on what?" Elizabeth asked coolly. "Your good looks?"

Mark lifted his chin. "Based on the fact that the guy who owns Bob Matthews Cars is an ex-basketball player. He likes jocks. My uncle helped me out with the down payment. Any more questions about my personal finances?" he asked aggressively.

He'd never liked Elizabeth much. He thought she was uptight, sanctimonious, and humorless. The type who was always sneering at people who weren't like her. She'd sure made a career of taking potshots at jocks—him included. When she'd gone public with the "special privileges scandal," she'd toppled his career as well as Todd's.

"Just one more question," Todd said in a low voice with very little expression. "You said nobody ever offered you money to play for SVU. Did anybody ever offer you money to lose?"

Mark felt his breath quicken, and his heart began to pound inside his chest. Elizabeth Wakefield was unbelievable. Didn't she ever give it a rest?

He couldn't believe the way they had manipulated him into coming back to SVU. Wilkins had said he was trying to clear things up. Get them back on the team. And it had been a lie. What they wanted was to crucify Mark Gathers completely.

He tried to restrain himself, but he couldn't. Something inside Mark snapped and he dove for Todd, knocking the table over and spilling the coffee in every direction.

Lila dropped the scrub brush and ran her finger along the bottom of the enormous, old-fashioned bathtub that stood high off the floor on four claws. There was still a thick layer of green on the pipes and fixtures where the copper had oxidized. And there was some kind of crystallized buildup around the drain that she hadn't been able to remove. But at least the remaining crud was sterile, and the cracked yellow tiles of the floor had been swept and mopped.

Beads of sweat dripped down Lila's brow. She'd never cleaned a bathroom before in her life—and as far as she was concerned, if she never did it again, it would be too soon.

But after a night spent changing buckets, mopping up the mess from the leaky roof, and sleeping on that old foam-rubber mattress that raised a cloud of dust every time she turned over, Lila felt dirtier than she'd ever felt in her whole life.

Bruce had gone to his morning class. Lila had decided to skip hers, clean out the tub, and take a long, hot soak in some of her expensive bubble bath.

She leaned over and turned on the faucets. A stream of hot water spewed into the old bathtub. Just out of curiosity, she leaned down and peered under the tub.

She recoiled in disgust. There was stuff growing up. Stuff growing down. Bleeeeh!

As soon as there was some cash, they needed to get a cleaning team in here.

She stripped off her filthy cotton pants and expensive silk T-shirt, both of which were ruined beyond repair. She poured a generous amount of bubble bath into the water.

135

With pleasure, she watched the water level rise. These old tubs had their good points. They were long and deep. Perfectly designed for self-indulgent soaking.

She lifted her ponytail, pinned it to the top of her head, and climbed into the tub. "Ahhhhh," she sighed, leaning back. As the soft, warm water closed around her, the horrendous events of the previous night began to recede.

It was a beautiful morning. The sun was shining. Bruce had spoken with Mrs. Finch and been assured that workmen would arrive this afternoon to connect the telephone and repair the roof.

Once those things were taken care of, Lila felt sure that they could make themselves happy here. They had each other. They had their privacy. They had a challenge to meet together.

They were broke, so they were learning to live like other people lived.

It was romantic. It was an adventure. It was . . . getting awfully cold.

Lila held her hand under the stream gushing from the faucet. It was ice cold. She turned off the cold tap, leaving only the hot water on.

The "hot" water was just as icy cold as the cold water.

With a gasp of impatience, she jerked the handles, shutting off all the water. What good was a deep-soaking tub if there wasn't enough hot water to fill it?

She lay back down, determined to enjoy what

remained of the warm water in the tub.

Suddenly the door opened with a loud bang, and heavy footsteps entered the apartment. Lila sat up and screamed when a large bearded workman wearing a tool belt and faded plaid shirt appeared in the doorway.

Immediately he backed up and out of sight. "Sorry, ma'am. I didn't realize there was anybody in the apartment."

"Who are you?" she demanded.

"I'm here to fix your roof."

"Now? We told Mrs. Finch we'd be out this afternoon."

"Mrs. Finch just left for the bus station," the man explained. "She gave me the passkey."

"You mean she's gone out of town? She didn't say anything about going out of town."

"Her sister's on a bender again. I mean, she's ill and . . ."

"When is she coming back?"

"Next week. Maybe."

Lila sighed impatiently. It was Mrs. Finch's job to arrange for repairs and supervise workmen. Not hers. "Well, I'm in the bathtub right now," she said irritably. "Can you come back later?"

"Sorry. I've got a solid work schedule."

There was a rap on the door, more footsteps, and then a second male voice. "SVC Tel. You got a phone problem?"

Lila sank down farther into the suds. "Our phone won't work," she called out.

"That's because you haven't paid the bill," the second voice said cockily.

"We just moved in," Lila retorted indignantly. How dare this guy imply that she was a deadbeat?

"If you say so. I still need a check for two hundred and thirty-four bucks before I can hook it up."

"But we just moved in!"

"You got anybody around here that can vouch for you? What about the landlady?"

"She's out of town."

"Lady," the first workman continued, "if you want me to fix that roof today, I gotta get started."

"Lady, if you want your phone fixed, I gotta get a check from you before I hook it up."

Lila groaned and slumped down under the suds.

Tom Watts sat in the conference room of the enormous and plush Las Vegas Uptown Hotel along with about fifty other student broadcast journalists from around the country.

The conference room was large, spacious, and contemporary. Tom felt very professional sitting in his black leather and chrome chair. In fact, the students were being treated so professionally he was glad he'd worn gray slacks, a blazer, and loafers instead of jeans and athletic shoes. It made him feel more businesslike.

The chairs were arranged in five rows of ten, facing a podium. In the back, long bleached-wood conference tables held pitchers of water, urns of coffee, and cans of soda for the participants.

At a podium in the front of the room a representative of UBC, University Broadcasting Company, was giving a presentation on their new service. The presentation was just one of several seminars and meetings that had been scheduled.

Tom uncrossed his long legs, stretched them, and then recrossed them at the knee. Usually it was hard for him to sit comfortably for long periods. He was athletic and used to moving around. But the conference was so interesting that for once, sitting for a long time didn't bother him.

UBC was a new closed-circuit cable channel devoted to NCAA sports coverage. It was the first station of its kind and Tom, along with most of the other visiting student journalists, was excited about the possibility that the channel might expand its programming to cover not just sports—but also news and social issues that related to college life.

If it did, it meant they would accept stories from student broadcasters. Local pieces shot on video that would receive closed-circuit broadcasting on all subscribing campuses.

Tom looked again at the elaborate press package that had been prepared. Then he felt a stab of guilt.

Elizabeth would love to be here. She'd love meeting colleagues from all over the country, attending the workshops, and sitting up late in the coffee bar, talking shop.

She'd get a lot out of it, but she'd put a lot into it, too. Elizabeth was the kind of person who always gave a hundred and fifty percent and never counted her change.

But instead of being here, she was back on campus, poring over dull financial records, putting together a routine story about fund-raising. It was a dull assignment—that was why she was coming up with all kinds of wild theories about payments to players from mysterious alumni.

He pressed his lips angrily. She hadn't come up with that cockamamie story on her own. She'd had help.

Tom had mixed feelings about Todd Wilkins. Sometimes he was an okay guy. But Tom knew Todd still had a major grudge against the university over they way it had treated him. If Todd could make trouble for the athletics department, he'd probably do it. He wasn't above getting Elizabeth to help him, either.

Tom uncrossed his legs again, growing restless. He wished he had been more tactful when he'd told her to back off and do the story she had been assigned.

Stop feeling guilty, he ordered himself. He had to learn to stop blaming himself all the time. He was the senior person at the station. It didn't matter that Elizabeth was his girlfriend. And it didn't matter whether or not Elizabeth was bored with the story.

When it came to the station, he was the boss. That meant it was his job to be here and it was her job to be there.

He'd been right to tell her back off. And right to do it in a way that left absolutely no doubt in her mind about who was boss. He was absolutely, positively, indisputably right!

Why is there so little satisfaction in being right? he wondered, no longer comfortable in his seat. He wasn't just feeling restless. He was feeling guilty . . . guilty . . . guilty.

He couldn't stand it anymore. There was a bank of telephones in the lobby. He'd call Elizabeth and apologize for coming down so hard on her. "Excuse me. Excuse me," he whispered as he tried to unobtrusively thread his way down the row.

He left the room through a side door, hurried down a long hallway, and took a right, entering the lobby. It was large and brightly lit, with several seating areas. Around the huge perimeter were two coffee shops, a gift shop, a pharmacy, and a newsstand.

A large bank of telephones stood just a few feet away. He hurried to one of the telephones, punched in the numbers of his student-issued calling card, and dialed. There was no answer and after several rings, Elizabeth's machine answered.

"Hi! This is the machine for Elizabeth and Jessica. We're not in right now, but if you'll leave your name and number, one of us will return your call as soon as possible." The message was followed by a shrill beep.

Tom swallowed his disappointment. "Hi," he said in as cheerful a tone as he could muster. "It's me, Tom. Just calling to say . . ." He trailed off and coughed. He didn't want to leave a flowery message on the machine where Jessica might hear it. "Just calling to check on how things are going at the station. Hope the work's not too dull."

Should he tell her he loved her? No. That was too private to say to an answering machine. "I'll call you back soon," he said. "Bye." He replaced the receiver with a soft click and fought the feeling of faint depression he always felt when he was away from Elizabeth.

According to the clock on the wall, the seminar would be over in five minutes. There was no sense disturbing everyone again by going back in. He'd just sit in the lobby and people-watch until it was time for the next meeting.

He wished Elizabeth were here to enjoy the spectacle with him. Las Vegas attracted every conceivable type of visitor. Couples who came to be married in Elvis chapels. Little old ladies who stood for hours in front of the slot machines. Paunchy middle-American tourists in pastel warm-up suits and expensive jogging shoes. Entertainers—male and female—with big hair.

There were some terrific acts playing in every hotel and club on the strip. The UBC executives were taking everybody out to dinner tonight and then to a show. Everything was first class, glamorous, and perfect.

Unfortunately, without Elizabeth it wasn't any fun.

Chapter Thirteen

"Jessica!"

Jessica turned and saw Isabella hurry up the wide hallway of the language arts building. She seemed to be trying to catch up with her. Isabella's shoulder-length dark hair swung back and forth, catching the light as she jogged. Her high-heeled boots made a tapping sound on the marble floor. "Are we late?" she panted, falling into step beside Jessica.

"What do you mean, we?" Jessica frowned. "You're not in this class."

Isabella giggled. "Ever since Professor Miles joined us for breakfast the other day, I've had an amazing interest in medieval history. So do Alison, Magda, Kimberly and Tina."

When Jessica didn't smile, Isabella knit her brows in confusion. "Remember? At breakfast. He said we could all sit in on a class if we wanted to."

"Oh, yeah, right." Jessica tried to look amused, but she felt slightly alarmed and annoyed. She had hoped she'd get a few minutes to talk to Louis after class. There was no way he'd talk to her with Alison and the other girls hanging around.

Isabella looked at her watch. "Come on. We've got two minutes." She took Jessica's sleeve and began dragging her toward the auditorium-style lecture hall. "You don't look so good," Isabella commented bluntly as they entered the room and looked around for a place to sit. "Are you sick?"

"I couldn't sleep last night," Jessica answered briskly as Isabella pulled her toward the two available seats behind Alison, Kimberly, Tina, and Magda.

"No, they can't," Alison Quinn was saying in a loud whisper.

"Yes, they can," Magda insisted.

"Can what?" Isabella asked, leaning forward to join their conversation.

"Teachers can date students, can't they?" Magda asked.

"Not if they want to keep their jobs," Isabella said. "Last year one of the girls in Chi Phi dated a teacher and there was a huge scandal about it."

"Did he get fired?" Magda pressed.

Jessica felt her stomach ball into a knot as she waited for the answer. But instead of an answer, Isabella let out a little giggle. "Thinking about dating Professor Miles?" she teased.

Alison blushed and grinned. "Isn't everybody?"

"He is gorgeous, isn't he?" Isabella purred. "And so deliciously unavailable."

The girls all giggled, and Jessica's throat tightened. She wished the class would begin so they would shut up.

"What do you think, Jessica? Still determined to stay out of love?" Isabella teased.

All the girls laughed again, and Jessica felt her lower lip trembling. She was dangerously close to tears.

Isabella was one of the kindest people she had ever met, besides her sister. The only thing that kept Jessica from bursting into sobs was the knowledge that Isabella had no idea she was being cruel. She would be horrified if she realized her remarks were like a knife twisting in Jessica's heart.

Somehow Jessica managed to stretch her lips into something that resembled a smile. "More determined than ever." She had to force the words through her constricted throat.

"Shh . . . Here he comes."

Alison and Magda turned to face the front, and the rest of the students fell silent as Professor Miles came striding through the side door with a hurried gait.

Louis looked slightly disheveled. As if he'd slept in his clothes, arrived late, and run across campus with his books and papers spilling out of his briefcase.

He didn't greet the class with a smile and a joking remark as he usually did. Instead he

145

dropped his case on the desk and began to sort through the papers.

Some people talked quietly while they waited for him to begin the class. Next to her Jessica felt Isabella restlessly rustle the pages of her textbook. In front of her she saw Magda and Alison put their heads together and begin a conversation.

Slowly the quiet hum in the room rose until the noise level was loud enough to attract Louis's attention. Louis angrily looked up. "Quiet," he barked.

For a split second, his gaze held Jessica's. Then it shifted away and scanned the stunned, silent class, as if rebuking them for their rudeness.

"Wow!" Isabella exclaimed under her breath. "He's even more beautiful when he's angry."

Jessica could feel Isabella's eyes on her, waiting for her to giggle. But she kept her eyes on Louis.

He turned his attention back to his papers, found what he wanted, then walked to podium. "It is often said that chivalry is dead," he announced. "I'm not sure that's true. But we cannot debate the question without first understanding what it is that has supposedly died. What is chivalry? What did it mean in the Middle Ages? What does it mean now?"

Jessica watched his face intently for the next forty minutes while he lectured on the subjects of honor, chivalry, and courtly love.

The unhappy ache in Jessica's heart began to fade away. By the end of the class, it had been replaced with a hot, burning fury. How dare he talk about honor? How dare he talk about courage? What would he know about chivalry or courtly love?

Her contempt was so profound, she felt like throwing her book at him. How could he be such a hypocrite? What kind of code did he live by? The code of weasels?

Louis had no honor. And no loyalty, either. He was a coward who was too afraid of losing his job to take a chance on love.

If that was the code of the knights, they could keep it.

"Okay. That ought to do it." The workman raised his arm and gave the wet plaster on the ceiling a final stroke. "If it doesn't hold, give me a call." He plucked a card from the breast pocket of the flannel shirt that stretched across his wide chest and even wider stomach and handed it to Lila with a leering wink. "Call me anyway."

Lila gave him a tight smile. "I'll give this to my boyfriend. He's usually the one who deals with repairs."

The workman gave her another wink and rested his bushy beard on his chest while he scribbled on his clipboard. "I'll give you a copy of the bill so you can get reimbursed by Mrs. Finch." He tore off the bill and held it out to her.

"Oh," she gasped, realizing he was giving it to her to pay. "I'm so sorry. I . . ." She let out an embarrassed laugh. The words she was about to say had never passed her lips before. "I don't have any money."

The workman's eyes darted around the apartment, and he grinned. "I'll bill Mrs. Finch directly." He looked around again, studied the furniture, and appeared to reach a decision. "Here." He reached into his pocket. "You and the boyfriend get a burger on me." He pressed a ten-dollar bill into her hand.

Lila felt her jaw drop, and she sucked in her breath with an insulted gasp.

"No, no. Don't thank me. I was young myself once."

Before Lila could clarify her feelings, he had backed out the door and closed it.

Lila stared at the money, torn between anger, amusement, and gratitude. Then she lifted the bill and felt a tear running down her cheek.

What an incredibly kind thing to do.

No one would ever think to do something like that for the rich Lila Fowler. She went to the window and watched the workman's bulky body as he lumbered down the front walk toward his truck. She didn't despise him anymore. She didn't resent the wink or the come-on or the intrusion. He was just a very nice man who'd tried to help her.

Was this what the real world was like? A planet overflowing with ordinary people who had an extraordinary capacity for kindness?

When she turned around, the little apartment

was transformed. No longer did she see a make-shift hovel with peeling wallpaper, chipped paint, and a newly plastered ceiling.

It really was the love nest she had dreamed of. A home where she and Bruce could learn not only about each other, but also about life.

Singing happily, Lila began to remove her clothes again. She was filthy and dirty and cold. She needed a long soak. So what if there was no hot water? Thinking good thoughts would keep her warm.

Even though the bathroom floor had been cleaned, it was still slightly gritty. She tiptoed across it. A cold draft came whistling through the door, causing her to shiver when she leaned over to turn on the faucet.

There was a great groaning noise inside the pipes. It sounded like a train roaring by and then disappearing off into the distance.

Lila sank to the floor and groaned as loudly as the pipes.

There was no hot water.

There was no cold water.

There was no water at all.

Winston stood in the clump of trees on the edge of the visitors' parking lot as he watched his parents pull in. They had come in the Suburban, he noticed. It was a big vehicle. Plenty big enough to cart Winston and all his junk back home.

Do people ever run away and join the circus any-

more? he briefly wondered. This was the most agonizing thing he'd ever been through. He'd much rather face down a man-eating tiger than look his father in the eye and see the disappointment there.

Mr. Egbert climbed out of the car. From where Winston stood, he looked as if he had aged fifteen years. And when he walked around the car and helped Winston's mother from her seat, she moved like someone who had been ill.

Winston hadn't spoken to his father yet. Only with his mother. The school had called and, according to Mom, Mr. Egbert was too upset to speak over the phone. Apparently she was too, because after moaning, "Winston how could you?" she had lapsed into incoherent tears.

Fortunately Winston had been able to ascertain the time and place of the meeting with Professor Stark and Dr. Stratton, head of the Freshman Disciplinary Council.

The time was now.

The place was here.

Winston slapped his thighs, brushing off any dust that might be clinging to his jeans. He adjusted the blue-and-red-striped tie he wore with his white shirt and navy blazer. Expulsion was probably a pretty formal affair, he figured.

Winston walked into Dr. Stratton's office, his heart in his throat, a few minutes after his parents entered. The first face he saw was his father's. It was the saddest face he had ever seen. And the angriest.

The impact was so fierce, Winston's knees turned to jelly. He fell, rather than sat, into the chair that Dr. Stratton offered.

"Winston," Dr. Stratton began in a dry, stern tone. "I've been telling your parents that Sweet Valley University has a very strict policy about cheating."

Winston swallowed and felt the blood draining from his cheeks.

"Cheating is not tolerated, and I'm sure you can understand why."

Winston looked at his mother. Her mouth was trembling, and she put a hand on Mr. Egbert's sleeve.

Winston lowered his eyes and stared at the tips of his boots. This was worse than he thought. The only thing that could possibly make this more grotesque would be if Denise were in the room too.

No need to worry about that, though. She hadn't spoken to him since he'd broken the bad news.

"However," Dr. Stratton continued, "in instances involving freshmen of otherwise good standing and impeccable high school records, I have a certain amount of latitude."

Winston jerked up his head. Latitude? Latitude as in, let's just forget this ever happened? They never could, of course. But it would be nice to try.

"What are you suggesting?" Mr. Egbert asked.

"I'm suggesting that we put Winston on probation for the rest of the academic year. If there are no further incidents, and I'm sure there won't be, I think we can erase this episode from his permanent record. Winston is well regarded and a good student. I'd like to see him have another chance."

If Dr. Stratton weren't so forbidding looking, Winston would have thrown himself across the room and hugged him. "Thank you," he croaked. "Thank you so much, sir."

"Not so fast!" Mr. Egbert said abruptly, holding up his hand.

The two professors lifted their eyebrows in surprise.

"You're going to let him off just like that?" Mr. Egbert demanded in an outraged tone.

"Dad!" Winston protested.

"You're just going to slap him on the wrist and tell him not to do it again?"

Winston bulged his eyes in his mother's direction, wordlessly begging her to call off the old man. But Mrs. Egbert didn't exert any restraining influence. She simply glowered in Winston's direction.

"What kind of lesson are you teaching him?" Mr. Egbert exploded. "If his actions don't have painful and unpleasant consequences, where is the incentive not to do it again?"

"Dad!" Winston cried, jumping to his feet. "What are you trying to do? Get me tarred and feathered?"

"I'm trying to make you a man!" his father

yelled back, standing up and waving his arms. "I want you to grow up and learn to be responsible."

That's when Mrs. Egbert jumped in with both feet, looking so angry that Winston reared back, fearful that she was about to let fly with some serious pocketbook action.

Make him a man! Winston thought wildly. What was with this "be a man stuff" all of a sudden? That had been Denise's big exit line too. "Be a man, why don't you?" she had said in a voice of withering contempt.

Dr. Stark jumped up and inserted himself between Winston and his parents. It was a small office, and if things got any more out of hand, there was liable to be some breakage.

He and Dr. Stratton both began making soothing, tsking noises at his parents, and Winston retired to a corner, feeling like exactly what he was—a guy whose own parents had turned on him.

"I understand your concerns, Mr. Egbert. But what do you suggest?" Dr. Stratton asked, coaxing Winston's father back into a chair.

"ROTC!" Mr. Egbert replied. "The Reserve Officers' Training Corps."

"The army!" Winston squeaked.

"Discipline. Teamwork. Citizenship," Mr. Egbert said, practically smacking his lips with satisfaction as he said the words. "Winston, your character needs molding."

"It's moldy enough already," Winston shot

back. "I think the fact that I'm here proves that." He laughed weakly, hoping his little joke would dispel some of the tension and make everybody see what a perfectly ridiculous idea it was.

He looked around the room.

Nobody was laughing, and Winston began to get the uncomfortable feeling that like it or not, he was about to become all that he could be.

Chapter Fourteen

Tom lay on the bed in his hotel room and moodily clicked his way through the forty or fifty cable channels the hotel offered. The room was strewn with gifts and press materials, and Tom turned the complimentary UBC baseball cap backward on his head as he ate the last of the fancy macadamia nuts.

It was late afternoon, and the seminars were over for the day. He was on his own until the dinner.

His thumb quickly hit the clicker five times, and Lucille Ball, Lassie, a fat chef, and a comic skidded by in rapid succession before the picture came to a stop on a popular talk show. He punched the Off button.

It was hard to believe he was actually bored in Las Vegas. But he was. He missed school. He missed the station. And he missed Elizabeth.

155

Tom reached for his laptop and reviewed the notes he had prepared for his interview with Craig Maser. Since Tom was the SVU representative and Craig Maser was an SVU student, Tom was scheduled to do a piece on him.

The review confirmed what he already knew. His notes were in good shape. There was nothing else to do to prepare—at least not until the athletes arrived.

He reached for the phone and dialed Elizabeth again. He'd tried her two more times that afternoon, but she'd been out. The phone rang three times before she answered it. "Hello?"

"I miss you," he said without preamble.

"Tom?"

He laughed. "Who else calls to say they miss you?"

He expected a laugh and a snappy comeback. But she simply grunted at her end of the line. Tom could hear the click, click, click of the keypad. She was angry.

"Liz, I'm sorry I was rude. And I'm sorry I didn't apologize sooner, but I couldn't get you on the phone, and I didn't want to leave a personal message on your machine."

"It's okay," she said briskly. "Don't worry about it."

"I'm going to worry about it if you're mad at me."

"I'm not mad. I'm just busy." He could hear her sliding the keypad away and turn her attention from the computer to the phone. Her voice became more focused. "I'm not angry. I'm just really involved in a project here. Don't be so sensitive."

"What's so absorbing?" he asked.

"What else? The story on alumni donations. Isn't that what you told me to do?"

Tom sighed unhappily. Clearly she was still peeved, and she wasn't ready to let it go. "I'll let you get back to your work, then," he said in a joking tone. "I know it's fascinating."

He was rewarded by a preoccupied laugh. "It is."

"I miss you," he said again.

"I miss you too," she said. She sounded sincere, but he still had the uneasy sense that he didn't have her full attention. "Elizabeth," he said, trying to keep his voice neutral. "Have you seen much of Todd lately?"

"Why do you ask?"

Because you loved him for most of your life, and I can't ever forget that. Especially when things between us aren't perfect. "No reason," he said lightly. "I just hate for you to be bored. I know that Todd's an old friend and . . ." He trailed off, realizing how transparent his question had been. "Never mind. I'm sorry I asked. Take care, sweetie. I'll call you later. Bye-bye."

"You take care too," she responded. "And don't bet on the horses," she joked before hanging up.

Tom smiled and replaced the receiver. His fingers idly untwisted the knots in the curling telephone cord. Elizabeth might not be mad, but she wasn't thrilled with him, either.

Tom picked up the remote control and turned the TV back on. *I'm never leaving town on a bad note again,* he vowed.

"Did he sound suspicious?" Todd asked.

Elizabeth stared intently at the screen as the names, figures, and statistics she'd compiled scrolled across it. "A little," she said. "But he's such a tyrant at the station, I don't think it occurs to me I wouldn't do what he told me to do."

Todd leaned over her shoulder to peer more closely at the monitor. "If you were smart, you would."

"Look who's talking. I'm not the one who told off Santos. That wasn't very smart, was it?"

"No," Todd said. "It wasn't. Stop! There it is." Todd pointed at the screen. "Chuck Hooper."

Elizabeth tapped a key on the computer and froze the screen.

Todd whistled. "Look at that record. Now see how many match it."

Elizabeth tapped another key and a list of names popped up on the screen along with their high school and college scoring records. To the left, the statistics arranged themselves on a graph.

The curser moved up and down a list of names and settled on one, JIM GUTHRIE. Todd picked a pencil and paper up off the desk and made a note of the address.

Elizabeth tapped the scroll key again and the name Daryl Cartright appeared with a strip of highlighting over it. They looked at each other and smiled. "Now tell us something we don't know," Todd said to the computer with a laugh.

Elizabeth leaned back in her chair and stretched. "I never could have put all this together without the sports data Gin-Yung had in her head. She's truly unbelievable."

Todd pulled Jessica's desk chair over and sat down next to Elizabeth so that he could reach the keypad. "When you see it put together like this, the pattern just jumps out." He ran his hands through his hair and exhaled deeply. "What if we took this to the federal authorities and showed it to them? They'd have to do something. I mean, it's right there. You can't miss it."

"These are just statistics," Elizabeth argued, exiting the program. "Statistics can be made to prove anything. And statistics don't testify. We need a witness. Somebody who can tell us, and the federal authorities, exactly what they were paid to do and who paid them to do it." She lifted a pencil and poked impatiently at her ponytail. "Too bad Mark Gathers didn't come through with the answers we wanted. I was hoping he'd be the key to unlocking this mystery."

Todd reached into his jacket and pulled out his car keys. "Come on."

"Where are we going?"

"Let's talk to Daryl Cartright again."

"He won't talk," Elizabeth said.

"I have a feeling he's dying to talk," Todd said. "But he's afraid to. Let's see if we can find out why."

Elizabeth stared significantly at the swollen black eye Mark had given him. Todd laughed, reading her mind. "Don't worry. I'll keep my head low. Besides, Daryl doesn't look to me like the type to hit."

"He doesn't look like the type to throw a game, either," she said cynically. "But we both know he did."

Chapter Fifteen

Daryl was in the driveway sinking baskets when Elizabeth and Todd drove up to his house. When he noticed them turn into his drive, Daryl's face turned cold, and he tucked the ball under his arm.

"He doesn't look happy to see us," Elizabeth said.

"What are you doing here?" Daryl asked in an unfriendly tone as they got out of Todd's car.

"We wanted to talk to you a little bit more," Todd said in a relaxed, friendly tone.

"I've got nothing to say."

"Then just listen," Todd suggested. He leaned against the front of the car and crossed his arms over his chest. "Here's the way I see it. Somebody offered you a lot of money to fumble the ball and shave some points here and there. You needed the money, and you took it. You weren't threatened and you weren't coerced, so even if you talked to

161

the federal authorities, you don't really have an acceptable excuse, do you? So what would you stand to gain by testifying? Nothing, except the possibility of a criminal indictment."

"Man," Daryl said, bouncing the ball and shaking his head. "You've got a great imagination. You ought to be a writer with a good imagination like that."

"I'm the writer," Elizabeth said. "But I'm a journalist. That means I'm interested in facts, not fiction. Are those the facts?"

Daryl threw down the ball and took a step forward with clenched fists. "Why should I tell you anything?"

"Because deep down, most people are more comfortable telling the truth," Todd said kindly. "And you're no different."

"Get out of here!" Daryl shouted.

"You've given up," Todd argued. "But maybe it doesn't all have to be over. Maybe something can be worked out. A lot of times federal witnesses get immunity from prosecution. But nothing can be worked out until you're willing to be honest."

"Leave me alone!" Daryl yelled.

"What are you afraid of? Who are you afraid of?"

"Man! I'm not afraid of anything. Or anybody, either."

"Then why won't you tell me?" Todd pressed. "Because they paid for some medical treatment for your sister? That's done. You got what you

162

wanted. They got what they wanted. You don't owe them anything anymore. The deal's over."

"No, it's not," Daryl exploded. "They paid and they're still paying, okay? We go to the top specialists, and the bills get paid."

"Will you tell the authorities that?" Elizabeth asked softly.

"No," Daryl said curtly. "I won't. Not in a million years." He whirled around and walked into the small house through the kitchen door.

Todd jerked his head, and the two of them followed him in. Daryl turned and glared. "Didn't anybody ever teach you to knock?"

"You're not the only one, Daryl. There are lots of guys out there in the same bind."

Daryl shrugged. "That's their problem. Not mine. Not yours, either. People do what they have to do. Don't judge."

"I'm not judging you, man," Todd insisted quietly. "Believe me, I'm the last guy in the world to judge anybody. I'm trying to help you."

"I don't need any help."

"Yeah, you do," Todd argued, shoving his hands in his pockets and leaning against the counter. "You're trying to be mother and father to two brothers and a sister, and you've got no job prospects. You need to go back to school. But you can't go back to school without a scholarship."

"A scholarship won't make any difference." Daryl snorted. "Everybody's always saying the only way out is go to school. School? Who's got time for school? I'm running around twenty-four hours a day, trying to keep up with those kids. You can't imagine what it's like to raise these kids. I've got to deal with gangs, drugs, guns, liquor."

Todd saw his throat quiver.

"I've got to be here," Daryl choked. "I'm the only thing standing between those two boys and all the mess out there." A silver tear left a glistening trail along Daryl's cheek.

"What about the future?" Elizabeth asked softly, laying a hand on his arm. "Where are you going to go from here without an education?"

Daryl shook off her hand with a tired gesture. "I can't think about the future," he said hoarsely. "I can only take things one day at a time. And today, the doctor is paid." He walked over to the door and yanked it open. "Good-bye," he said. "And please, please, please don't come back."

Tom tightened the knot on his tie and grimaced at his reflection in the mirror. There had been a note in Elizabeth's voice that was still bothering him.

He went to the telephone. Should he? Or shouldn't he?

He shouldn't, but he was going to. Tom reached for his telephone pad and found Gin-Yung's number. He dialed it quickly, before he could chicken out. She answered after two rings.

"Gin-Yung," he said pleasantly. "This is Tom Watts, calling from Las Vegas."

There was a surprised pause before she spoke. "Hi!" she responded.

"I, uh, just thought I'd call and . . . and . . ." He trailed lamely off.

He heard her laugh at the other end of the line. "I'm glad I'm not the only one with a suspicious mind."

"Are they spending a lot of time together?"

"Every minute," Gin-Yung answered sourly. "But Todd swears there's nothing going on between them. And so far, I believe him."

Tom sat down on the edge of the bed and fiddled with the phone cord. "So what are they doing?"

"I'm not supposed to tell," she said.

Tom rolled his eyes. "Oh, come on. We're all in the news business. You can tell me. They're chasing down some scandal, right?"

There was another long pause. This time, Gin-Yung's voice was serious. "Tom. You're putting me on the spot here. I promised Todd I wouldn't talk about what they're doing and . . ."

"Okay, okay. I understand," Tom said. The tight knots in his stomach were beginning to relax. Gin-Yung was as possessive as a pit bull. If she had her eye on the Todd-Elizabeth duo, he could relax. She'd intervene if she thought things were turning romantic. As far as the "story" Todd and Elizabeth were working on, the worst thing that would happen was that they would wind up wasting a lot of time and feel very foolish when he got back to SVU. "Gin-Yung. Do me a favor, will you?"

"I won't tell Elizabeth or Todd that you called," she said, anticipating his request.

"Thanks. And I'll see you in a few days." When he hung up the phone, he laughed out loud at his own arrogance. He was pretty sure Gin-Yung would keep her word. But if she didn't, and Elizabeth knew he'd been checking up on her and Todd, the one who was going to look foolish when he returned to SVU—was him.

"Is that him?" Elizabeth asked. A tall, good-looking guy with a blond ponytail appeared in the doorway of the two-story brownstone across the street. He carried a large portfolio under his arm.

"I think so," Todd answered. "I looked up his picture in an old yearbook. His hair wasn't as long a couple of years ago. But I think it's him."

It was nighttime and Elizabeth and Todd were in Fulton, a town an hour and a half away from SVU. They were standing on a sidewalk lined with quaint shops and restored buildings. Many of the shop windows displayed paintings and sculptures created by the students of the Fulton Fine Arts Institute—one of California's best art schools.

"Come on," Todd said. "Let's catch up with him at the corner."

Elizabeth and Todd kept several yards behind. They didn't want to alarm him and send him running. When he stopped for the light, they casually made their approach. "Chuck Hooper?" Elizabeth asked.

The guy turned, looked Elizabeth up and down, and gave her a curious smile. "That's right. Do I know you?"

"No. But I know you. We both do. I'm Elizabeth Wakefield, and this is Todd Wilkins."

"Todd Wilkins, Todd Wilkins, Todd Wilkins," Chuck repeated thoughtfully. "Wait a minute." He snapped his fingers. "You called me on the phone." His tongue pushed out his cheek as he thought about it. "Why are you here?" he asked, giving them a direct, but not unfriendly look.

He was wary, but he didn't seem the least bit alarmed, and Elizabeth wondered for a moment if she and Todd were both crazy. This time, she decided to use shock tactics. "To ask you if you ever got any money to shave points when you played for SVU," she said in a conversational tone.

"Point shaving!" Chuck repeated in mock exclamation. "That's illegal, you know."

"We know," Elizabeth said with a smile.

"Do you have any proof?"

"No. We were hoping you could help us."

"Sorry."

"Why not? We're not here to arrest you. We're here to help you if we can. If somebody took advantage of you or is exploiting you, maybe we can help."

Chuck smiled and tossed his long blond bangs

off his forehead. "I don't need any help. And no-body's exploiting me."

"But you're not playing basketball."

"Now ask me if I care." Chuck laughed.

"Do you care?" Elizabeth asked obligingly.

"Not in the least," Chuck said mildly. "I never liked sports, but I was good at them. I wanted to major in art. My father said no way. He wasn't going to pay for me to waste my time weaving baskets. So I went to SVU and enrolled in the business program, as per Chuck Hooper, Senior's, very explicit instructions." An angry shadow passed over Chuck Hooper, Junior's, serene brow, and Elizabeth sensed a deep animosity. "When you're the CEO of one of California's major busi-nesses, you're used to giving orders and having them carried out." There was bitter irony in his voice.

"I'm beginning to see the light," Elizabeth said. "Drop the ball and pick up a paintbrush at the Fulton Fine Arts Institute. All expenses paid. What's the worst thing that could happen? You'd get caught and your dad would be disgraced. A win-win situation."

Chuck smiled enigmatically. "You said it. I didn't." He grinned and winked. "And I never will." He gave Elizabeth an interested look. "I'm on my way to the campus gallery. I've got a show opening tonight. If you're free, drop by the recep-tion."

Chuck sauntered across the street without a

backward look, and Todd whistled through his teeth. "Santos is good. He figured out what these guys wanted and he gave it to them. No leaning. No threats. No leg breakers. No problem."

"It finally answers a question that's been bugging me for the longest time," Elizabeth said. "Why didn't anybody ever approach you?"

Todd nodded. "I guess I didn't have any easily identifiable area of vulnerability like these guys. No pressing needs or desires that they could exploit." He rubbed the back of his neck and sighed. "These guys sold their souls to the devil. Nobody's going to talk because everybody's happy with the deal."

"Everybody except Daryl," Elizabeth said quietly.

"He's getting what he wants."

"He's getting what he needs," Elizabeth said. "There's a difference."

"But Daryl's never going to tell anybody what's going on. You saw the way he was with those kids."

"So we have to figure out a way to offer him something he wants."

"Which would be . . . ?"

"His soul back."

"That's very poetic," Todd said with a dry laugh. "But too metaphoric for me. What are you talking about?"

"Daryl Cartright isn't happy about what he's doing," Elizabeth explained. "It's wrong, and he knows it's wrong. But he doesn't know how to stop doing it."

"And we would tell him . . . what?"

"I wish I knew," Elizabeth said with a sigh. "Come on. Let's go home. It's a long drive and I'm tired."

Chapter Sixteen

"No wonder you're so thin," Magda commented. "You haven't touched your food."

Several girls were gathered around the kitchen table at Theta house for dinner. Isabella had urged Jessica to join them for a late dinner of spaghetti and chocolate mousse cake. "You look almost as depressed as Denise," she had said. "You guys both need an evening with friends. It'll perk you up."

"What's wrong with Denise?" Jessica asked.

"I don't know. I guess we'll find out at dinner."

Jessica had reluctantly agreed to come. Now she wished she hadn't. Alison, Magda, Kimberly, and Tina had spent the entire time talking about guys. Jessica was sick of listening to them talk about who was dating who—and who wasn't dating who.

Worst of all, they were totally hooked on the subject of Professor Miles. They'd talked about him for almost an hour.

The phone rang, and Isabella jumped up. "Maybe that's Denise."

"Tell her if she doesn't hurry, she'll miss the mousse cake," Magda called out. She grinned at Jessica. "If you're not going to eat that, I'll finish it."

"Be my guest," Jessica said, trying hard to smile.

Magda whisked the plate of spaghetti away, and Alison gave Jessica a narrow look across the table. "So Jessica, what's wrong with you this evening? It's not like you to be so quiet."

Alison had never liked Jessica and in a million years, Jessica would never confide in her. She was small-minded, petty, jealous, and always looking for some way to get Jessica into trouble.

"I guess my mind is somewhere else," Jessica responded, trying to make her voice sound pleasant.

Usually just being in Theta house could improve Jessica's mood. She loved the elegant old house. The kitchen was large, with lemony yellow walls and dark mahogany cabinets. The adjoining living room was lovely and comfortable. Colorful throw rugs were scattered on the hardwood floors, making the room seem bright even on the dullest day. Jessica had spent many happy hours gossiping with friends while sprawled in an overstuffed chintz chair in front of the fireplace.

Tonight, though, the decor and the company felt fussy and suffocating.

"If your mind is somewhere else, that means it's on someone else," Magda teased. "Who is he?"

"There's nobody," Jessica said flatly. "And if you don't mind, I don't really feel like talking."

Alison rolled her eyes. "We've all been bummed out over guys before. You don't have to act like the tragedy queen of SVU."

That did it. "I'm out of here." Jessica stood up and left the table, striding through the living room and past Isabella just as she was hanging up the phone.

"Where are you going?" Isabella called out.

"To my dorm," Jessica said angrily.

"Wait." Isabella hurried after her, catching up with her on the porch and holding on to her arm.

"Back off," Jessica snapped.

Isabella fell back, and her mouth dropped open in astonishment. "Jessica!" she gasped. "What's with you? It's me, Isabella. Your best friend."

Jessica lowered her eyes and felt ashamed. Isabella was worried about her. But she couldn't tell Isabella what was wrong. "I just need to go back to my dorm, okay? Tell Denise I'm sorry I missed her."

"Denise isn't coming," Isabella said. "She's too upset. She's even thinking of leaving school. She and Winston have broken up."

"What!"

"Don't tell anybody else this, but Winston got caught cheating on his physics exam."

"Oh, no!" Jessica gasped.

"He was almost kicked out of school."

"Why would he do something like that?" Jessica cried.

"According to Denise, he did it because he was flunking physics. He was afraid his parents would send him to a smaller school, and he and Denise wouldn't be together anymore." Isabella shook her head in dismay.

"He did it for her," Jessica said, her voice breaking.

"Isn't that horrible?"

"No," Jessica cried. "I don't think it's horrible."

"Jessica!"

"This is the first thing he's ever done that makes me respect him," Jessica practically shouted in a defiant voice. "He did it because he was afraid of losing her. He was willing to take a chance on getting into trouble so he could be with her."

"He cheated," Isabella said. "Don't you get that?"

"What I get is that he was willing to risk something important for love. And if Denise doesn't get that, she's a fool." Jessica turned and ran off into the night.

"Jessica! Jessica, wait!"

Isabella didn't understand and neither did Denise. Sure, what Winston did was wrong. But right or wrong, at least he was willing to gamble the only things he had—his honor and his education—for love. Louis didn't care enough about her to take any kind of a chance at all.

The wind was whipping across the dark, deserted campus. Black clouds blotted out the moon, and the air was heavy with moisture. Another tropical storm was brewing.

It was dark on the west walk of the quadrangle. Outside the life sciences building, Jessica didn't see the sawhorses and scattered building materials until she stumbled over them.

When she fell, she managed to break her fall with her arms, but she scraped her forehead on a piece of cracked pavement and let out a little cry of pain. She raked back her hair, gently feeling the abrasion. "Oh, no." Her fingers came away bloody. She lifted her shoulder and wiped the cut on the soft cloth of her white cotton boat-neck sweater. It was ruined now, but so what? Her whole life was ruined. She scrambled to her feet, determined to run to the dorm and lock out the world.

But no matter how hard she ran, or how far, Jessica knew she couldn't run from her feelings. Her deep rage. Louis Miles was a coward and a fraud. She wouldn't be able to rest until she told him exactly what she thought of him.

She reached into the pocket of her jeans and found the keys to the Jeep. A few minutes later, she was in the parking lot behind her dorm and climbing into the red vehicle that she shared with Elizabeth. She turned the key in the ignition, backing recklessly out of the parking spot.

A sharp turn of the wheel sent the Jeep careening around the corner with the tires squealing. By the time she was on the road, the black clouds above her had parted, and a torrential rain came pouring down.

Mark Gathers shivered in the front hall of the Santos mansion. It was dark, gloomy, and slightly damp. A huge clap of thunder made him jump. Jeez. What a depressing place. It looked like the Addams family lived here. If he had the kind of money Santos obviously had, he'd get himself something more cheerful.

"Mr. Santos will see you now." A tall man in a dark business suit materialized out of the shadows like an apparition. Mark jumped again. He began to wish he hadn't come. This place was giving him the creeps.

There was another rumble of thunder. A bright, jagged bolt of lightning streaked across the sky outside, briefly illuminating all the windows of the front hall.

The man in the business suit laughed and smiled at Mark. "Sort of like a horror movie, isn't it?" The remark and the smile made the guy seem normal. Mark's shoulders relaxed. "Come on," the man said. "The office is this way."

Mark's feet made no noise on the thick oriental rug that ran the length of the long hall. The man opened a set of heavy double doors and stood aside.

Mark entered cautiously, and the man in the business suit stepped in behind him and closed the doors.

"Mark Gathers. We meet at last." The voice was friendly and welcoming. Mark looked around the dark room, trying to find its source. A small, ordinary-looking man stepped out of the shadows. "Mr. Santos?"

"Call me T. Clay," he said, walking forward with his hand extended. He took Mark's hand in a fatherly grip with his right hand and put his left arm around his shoulders. "I can't believe we've never met face to face. I was delighted to get your call, son. Sit down. Sit down. Tell me what's on your mind."

Mark took a seat in one of the high-backed leather chairs, and Mr. Santos sat down opposite— so close that his knees were almost touching Mark's. Mark's eyes involuntarily turned in the direction of the man in the dark suit standing in the corner of the room. Mr. Santos caught the gesture. "That's Bobbo. Don't worry about him. He's one of us."

"One of us?"

Mr. Santos winked. "Yeah. He's a real sports fan. That's what we're here to talk about, right? Sports?"

"Yeah," Mark said. "I mean, me and sports. I was sort of hoping you could help me."

"You want back on the team, right?"

Mark nodded. "Right. And . . ."

"And?"

Mark flushed. "Things didn't go too well for me after I got suspended. I'd like to go back to school, but . . . well . . . I'd need some kind of a job, and I was hoping you could help me get one."

Mr. Santos sat back and gave Mark a level look. "What could you do?"

Mark met his gaze squarely. "Whatever it takes."

Mr. Santos smiled and pulled a cigar from his pocket. He put the cigar in his mouth, lit it, and took a few puffs. "You said over the phone that you had been talking to Todd Wilkins."

Mark nodded. "That's right."

"He tell you what he's doing?"

"Yes, sir."

"And you decided to come see me."

"That's right."

Mr. Santos puffed thoughtfully again. "Does he have any proof, Mark?"

"No, sir. Not as far as I know."

"He ask you if you knew anything?"

"Yes, sir." Mark felt a bead of sweat form along his hairline.

"What did you tell them?"

"I told him that I didn't know anything." He smiled slightly. "And then I hit Wilkins in the eye."

Mr. Santos threw back his head and laughed. "I don't like Todd Wilkins," he said. "Sounds to me like you don't like him either."

"No, sir," Mark answered. "I don't."

Mr. Santos smiled. "Mark. I think I could talk to Dr. Beal and find something for you. It might be a while before I can arrange to get you back on the team. But if things go well, and I'm convinced you're serious about your career, then I don't think it's out of the question."

Mark smiled. "That's great. I really appreciate this."

Mr. Santos leaned forward and opened a box. Mark's eyes nearly bulged out of their sockets. In the box were stacks of one-hundred-dollar bills. As casually as if he were handling tissues, Santos peeled off five hundred-dollar bills and handed them to Mark. "Here's your first week's pay."

Mark took the bills, folded them, and stuffed them into his shirt pocket. "Thank you."

"I'll call Beal. From now on, you're the official student assistant in the athletics department. I want you to hang around the teams. Get to know the guys again. Keep your eyes open, and if you see or hear anything you think I ought to know, I want you to tell me." He leaned forward. "Understand?"

Mark answered with a curt nod.

"Anybody asks you who you're working for, you tell 'em you're an employee of the school."

"Yes, sir."

"Any questions?"

"No, sir."

Mr. Santos smiled broadly and stood. When Mark rose, Santos put a hand on his arm and walked him toward the double doors. "Mark," he said in a low tone. "One more thing."

"Yes, sir?"

"If I find out you're not being one hundred percent honest with me, I'm going to be very, very disappointed." His hand tightened on Mark's arm like a vise.

"I understand, sir. I won't disappoint you."

179

The phone on the desk rang, and Bobbo moved to answer it. He said something into the receiver, then, "Mr. Santos, sir. It's for you."

Santos released his grip on Mark's arm, and Mark could feel the bruise marks forming already.

Bobbo came to take his place, smiling at Mark. "Come on. I'll show you out."

Behind him, Mark could hear Santos talking into the phone. "Yeah. Yeah. Yeah. What I want is this—there's a blond female freshman by the name of Wakefield. She drives a red Jeep. Find her and put a tail on her."

Chapter Seventeen

Jessica careened down the dark beach road. The road was wet, and it was hard to see where she was going. When the curve loomed up out of nowhere, she jerked the wheel, taking the turn on two tires.

She was too angry to feel fear, though. When the Jeep settled safely back on the road, Jessica pressed her foot even harder against the pedal.

The rain beat against the roof like angry fists. Jessica reveled in the sound, gripping the wheel tightly. It was about time she finally stood up for herself.

Jessica saw the condos up ahead. His was the second from the left in a row of five. Four of the condos were dark, but there was one dim light on in his.

The Jeep came to a skidding stop in the driveway. Jessica jumped out, lowering her head. The wind was blowing hard, and the rain seemed to be battering her from every direction.

She ran toward the condo, half blinded by the storm. By the time she hurried up the stairs and banged on the door, she was soaked to the skin. "Louis!" she yelled. "Louis, come out here!"

Jessica grabbed the knocker on the door with both hands. Breathing hard, she bashed it against the door as hard as she could before backing up.

"Damn!" she heard him say as he unlocked the door and opened it, leaving the chain on. His face registered shock when he saw her. "Jessica!"

Louis quickly closed the door, slid off the chain, and then opened it again. He grabbed her arm, pulling her inside before slamming the door shut behind her. "What are you doing here?" he demanded.

"I came to tell you you're a lousy hypocrite!" she shouted tearfully. "You don't know anything about honor. Or chivalry. Or love. Or me!"

His face contorted.

"You should have left me alone," she yelled. "But you didn't. Why didn't you stay out of my life? I . . . I hate you!" She lifted her hand, determined to slap him.

His hand came up and gripped her wrist. "Stop it," he said angrily. "You sound just like—" He broke off, and the look of anger on his face turned to sorrow. "Please," he said hoarsely. "Please stop it." He pushed her hand down to her side and released it.

Jessica's harsh words hung in the air, and she felt her face growing hot. He moved to the window and closed the curtains before turning to get a good look at her. "You shouldn't have come here," he said. He frowned suddenly and took her chin in a firm grasp. "What happened to your face?" he asked tersely. "Who did this?"

"Nobody did anything. I fell," she said, jerking her head away. Her fury had subsided and now she felt embarrassed. He'd thought she was an immature child before, and her behavior had just confirmed it. "You're right," she said. "I shouldn't have come. I'm leaving."

"Jessica, wait," he begged.

She froze as he came up behind her. "I wish I could make you understand."

"I understand," she said bitterly. "I understand that I'm not important in your life, and I never will be."

"You'll never know how important you are," he said. When he put his hands on her shoulders, a thrill of electricity raced down her spine. He turned her around and brushed some raindrops from her face. "What I said on the phone . . . I . . ."

"You what?" she asked softly.

"I . . ." His eyelids fluttered down, and so did Jessica's. His lips found hers, and she felt the line of his body curve against her own.

He never finished his sentence, but it didn't matter. She knew what he was trying to tell her. It was the same thing she'd been trying to tell him. And it couldn't be expressed in words.

Drip, drip, drip . . .

"Argghhhhh!" Bruce threw off the blanket and sat up with a roar. "That noise is driving me nuts. How am I supposed to sleep with this kind of racket?"

"Don't yell at me," Lila said, sitting up beside him. "It's not my fault."

"I thought you said the workman was here," Bruce said. "What was he doing if he wasn't fixing the leaks?"

"I guess these are all new leaks."

Bruce looked gloomily around the tiny bedroom filled with pots and pans. It was around two in the morning and every little droplet sounded like a cymbal crash. "Call the guy again in the morning," he said grumpily. "Tell him to come back and fix the rest of the leaks."

"You call the guy in the morning," Lila retorted angrily. "I've got classes."

"So do I."

"Tough!" Lila yanked the quilt and turned over, leaving Bruce uncovered. "And while you're at it, call the plumber, too. If I have to go one more day without a hot bath, I'm going to lose my mind."

Bruce yanked the quilt back so that he had enough to cover himself. "Quit complaining and give me credit for getting the water back on." He'd spent what seemed like an hour on the cruddy floor, twisting dirty old knobs and pipes

184

until he'd gotten the water flowing again. Having no prior plumbing experience, he actually felt pretty proud of himself.

But had he gotten one word of praise from Lila? No way. She just kept yakking and yakking about not having hot water.

"I can live without a lot of things, but hot water isn't one of them."

"Cold showers are better for you." Bruce couldn't help saying it—even though he knew it would just irritate her.

Lila turned over with an annoyed flop, pulling the quilt to her side of the bed again. Bruce's feet, which were very sensitive to cold, began to tingle. "Lila. Can I have some of that quilt?"

Grudgingly she fed him a couple of inches.

"That's not enough," he complained.

"I'm cold," she said.

"So am I."

"Tough," she said again.

He sat up. "I'm getting tired of hearing that."

She sat up, and he could see her eyes glaring at him through the dark. "Tough!" she said, one too many times.

Bruce picked up his pillow and whacked her over the head with it. Lila let out a shriek of anger, mixed with amusement, and then grabbed her own pillow.

Bruce ducked. Lila missed him on the swing but caught him on the recoil. "Oomph!" he said, laughing as the down-filled pillow thumped him softly on the head. "Truce," he said.

"No way," she argued, reaching for her other pillow and delivering a one-two pillow punch with each hand.

"This bed is too small for a pillow fight," he said.

"Tough!" She giggled, giving him a push and sending him tumbling onto the floor.

"Ouch!" The floor was hard and cold and definitely no place to sleep.

"Ahhhh," Lila cheered in a voice of mock triumph. She stretched out diagonally across the bed, making it impossible for him to get back in. "Mine," she purred. "All mine." She wrapped herself defiantly in the whole quilt and sighed.

Bruce reached up and grabbed her ankle, pulling her, the quilt, and the foam-rubber mattress off the bed.

"Nooooo!" Lila shrieked as she and the bedding landed in a heap on top of Bruce. A couple of pans rolled across the floor with a clatter.

Both of them broke into fits of uncontrollable giggles.

"Shut up!" they heard a deep voice yell below the floor. The order was followed by several thumps on the ceiling. "It's two A.M.!"

"Tough!" Bruce and Lila yelled back in unison. Then they threw the mattress back on the bed, jumped in, and huddled as close together as possible beneath the quilt.

"Las Vegas is like living in Alaska or Iceland," Christine Mulroney said. "You know, one of those

186

places where it's daylight for months at a time. It's two in the morning and you'd think it was two in the afternoon."

Tom sat in the hotel coffee shop with Christine Mulroney and four other student broadcasters from schools all over the country. They had just finished a two A.M. snack and were lingering over their coffee, talking shop, and watching the people come in and out of the hotel lobby.

Tom laughed. Christine was right. Las Vegas stayed open and busy twenty-four hours a day.

"Funny," he said. "It's as active as it was this afternoon. But it's not exactly the same crowd." His eyes flickered over some of the men who hurried in and out of the bars, elevators, and meeting rooms. Some were flashy and obnoxious. Some were quiet and reserved. But they all had a slightly nervous quality. Their eyes seemed to be looking everywhere at once.

"No," Bill Reynolds agreed. "These are the serious gamblers. The guys who are at it round the clock. The pros." He smiled around the table. "Anybody care to place a small wager on the Maser-Fisher bout?"

"I wonder what those guys consider a small wager?" Tom mused.

"Probably only two or three million," Bill responded.

Tom shifted uneasily. Gambling on college events seemed out of line somehow. It created an atmosphere that was less than appealing, and he couldn't help thinking that Las Vegas might not have been the best place to hold the event. College sports had enough trouble keeping its image clean. It didn't need a bunch of professional gamblers hanging around the fringes.

He rubbed his eyes and yawned, flipping the Off button on his brain. He was getting as bad as a first-year journalism student. They were always sure that there were conspiracies brewing behind every bush. This was Las Vegas. It was Disneyland for adults, and a great place to launch a new entertainment system. Las Vegas had the facilities to sponsor the conference and the hype factor that it took to raise an NCAA wrestling match to the status of a major event.

"Have you guys checked out the ballroom where the match is going to be?" Tom asked.

Christine shook her head. "I tried to get in there this afternoon, but they were still setting up. They didn't want anybody in there. I'd like to get a look at it. Want to walk over and see if we can poke around now?"

Tom reached into his pocket, removed some money, and left it on the table to cover his coffee. "Yeah. I'd like to see it." He nodded to the other guys. "See you in the morning."

They all lifted their hands in a weary wave and turned back to the remains of their doughnuts and pies. Tom draped his jacket over his arm, and Christine shrugged on her sweater. "I've heard a lot of good things about SVU's broadcast journalism

188

department," she said as they left the coffee shop.

"We do a good job," Tom said, leading her across the lobby and down the long, ornate hallway. "If I do say so myself. Mainly we're successful because we've got a great team. I'm supposedly the star broadcaster. But believe me, it takes a lot of talented people to make me look good. A lot of researchers and technical people and . . ." A picture of Elizabeth flashed in his mind, and he felt yet another pang of guilt.

"Hello?" Christine said, waving her hand in front of his eyes.

"Sorry," he said. "Just lost my focus for a minute."

"It's called Vegas Fatigue, and they say it goes away twenty-four hours after you leave the city."

He laughed and opened the door of the ballroom. Christine moved her hands around the wall until she located a large light panel. She flipped several switches, and they both gasped.

"Look at the size of this place. It's as big as our baseball field," she marveled.

In the center of the room was a large ring. Bleachers had been constructed around it. At every corner of the ring were spaces for cameras and mikes.

Lights had been mounted on tracks overhead and the far right wall held an amazingly complex deck of electronic broadcasting equipment. Tom immediately went over to take a look at it. "Wow! Can you imagine what it would be like to have this kind of equipment in our college stations?"

189

Christine ran a hand lovingly over a computerized bank with nine monitors across it. "Wouldn't you love a chance to direct an event with a setup like this?"

"Hey!" a voice said sharply. "Who are you?" A man in a suit stood in the doorway, frowning at them.

"We're student broadcasters," Tom said, instinctively moving in front of Christine.

"Get out," the man said rudely. "You're not supposed to be here."

"Are you an employee of UBC or the hotel?" Tom asked, his temper rising.

"Neither," the man said.

"Then who are you?" Tom asked bluntly. "And what are you doing in here?"

The man moved forward with a menacing step. Tom tensed, preparing for a lunge, when a second man materialized in the doorway.

"Max," the other man said with quiet authority.

Max didn't move and continued to stare at Tom. Tom met his gaze with an unwavering stare.

"You can go, Max. I'll take care of this."

Max backed slowly out of the doorway of the huge ballroom, and Christine emerged from behind Tom's broad back.

"I'm very sorry," the man said with a smile. "We have to hire freelance security people when we do big events like this. They're not always as polished as we'd like."

The man was smiling genially at both of them,

but something about him rubbed Tom the wrong way. His smile was insincere and flashy. Real Las Vegas. "Who's we?" he asked without smiling back.

The man's eyebrows rose slightly, obviously surprised that a college kid was pressing the issue. "I'm Paul Klaus," the man said, extending his hand to shake Tom's. "I'm in charge of coordinating the hotel and the promoters and the broadcasters. And you are . . . ?"

"Tom Watts and Christine Mulroney."

Paul smiled, draping one arm over Tom's shoulders and his other arm over Christine's. "Listen, Tom. Look for me before the broadcast, and I'll make sure you and Christine get good seats and interviews with some of the celebrities." He began walking them toward the door.

"There are going to be celebrities here?" Christine asked.

Paul lowered his voice as if he were explaining something very elementary. "This is Las Vegas. There's more top talent in this town than there is in Hollywood. Celebrities are everywhere, and lots of them are sports fans. They come to these big events because they like the publicity. But they're very choosy about who they talk to."

They were in the hallway now, and Paul released his hold on their shoulders. "Look for me before the match," he said again. Then he gave them a thumbs-up sign and a wink before retreating into the ballroom and closing the doors.

"Wow!" Christine breathed. "Was that luck or

what? If I get a couple of decent celebrity interviews out of this thing, I'll have a great audition tape."

"Did you notice he never did tell us who he worked for?"

Christine shrugged. "So?"

"So who is he?"

"There are so many people around this place, I lost track a long time ago. Come on. It's three A.M. and we've got early meetings tomorrow."

Chapter Eighteen

Elizabeth turned over for the five-hundredth time. It was useless. She was worried sick and hadn't been able to sleep all night. The sunlight was just beginning to break through the clouds, but for once Elizabeth took no pleasure in the sight.

Across the room, Jessica's bed was undisturbed. The heavy weight in Elizabeth's stomach grew even heavier. *Where is she?* When she'd gotten home late last night and there was no sign of Jessica, Elizabeth had been slightly worried. By midnight, she'd begun to create all kinds of possible scenarios. And by three, she was terrified.

Jessica wasn't involved in anything Elizabeth was doing. But somehow, Jessica always seemed to get drawn into Elizabeth's adventures and vice versa.

Adventures. Elizabeth grimaced as she stood up and went to the window. When they were in middle school, they'd had adventures. Now they were adults, and their "adventures" were fraught with dangers they had never dreamed of as children.

Was it possible that someone from Santos's group had confused Jessica and Elizabeth? It had happened before. Elizabeth took a deep breath, trying to calm herself. So far, she'd felt fairly safe. They hadn't found any proof yesterday. If Santos was in touch with Chuck, Santos knew that much. There was no need for him to take any action against Elizabeth or Todd. So why would he? Why do something illegal if he didn't have to? Santos was too smart to make a clumsy blunder like that.

But accidents could be arranged.

Had Jessica met with some kind of accident?

Elizabeth squeezed her hands together so tightly the nails dug into her palms. "Where are you?" she whispered, watching the rising sun illuminate the campus.

"You have to go now," Louis insisted. But even as he urged her to leave, he held Jessica tighter against his chest. Jessica wound her arms around his neck and rubbed her cheek against his morning stubble.

They stood at the door of the condo as Jessica prepared to leave. Over the top of her head, Louis could see the sun rising on the ocean through the living room window opposite.

All signs of last night's storm were gone and the sea was calm and flat, reflecting the pink-and-orange glare of a dawning new day.

"You don't really want me to go, do you?" she whispered in his ear.

He chuckled. "No, I don't. Why is it you always seem to know more about what I want than I do?"

"Because I love you," she said.

"And I love you too," he answered with no hesitation at all. He brushed his lips back and forth across hers. "But you really do have to go."

"Why do I have to go?" Jessica asked, lifting her lips to tempt him.

He kissed her hungrily, and it was several moments before he answered. "Won't someone be worried about you? Your sister?"

"I'll explain things to her," she said. "And . . ."

"No," he said, putting a finger to her lips. "Don't tell her anything."

"But Elizabeth is my sister. She'll understand."

"Please, Jessica. Promise me you'll keep our relationship a secret." He released her, opened the door a crack, and looked outside. "I wanted you to be gone before daylight," he muttered to himself. "Somebody might see you. Or your car."

Jessica planted her feet firmly. "I love you and I don't care if anybody sees me."

"But I do," he said, his face turning somber. "I love you too. But there are problems."

"I know your job is important to you. I understand that, and I don't want you to get into trouble because of me. But last night, you said you wanted me in your life. Isn't that still true this morning?"

The words were simple and childlike, but she

said them with a vulnerability that wrung his heart. Louis took her hands and gazed into her eyes. "Of course it's true. It'll be true every morning of my life. I'll work out the problems. I promise. But I need you to give me a little time. Okay?"

Louis opened the door, and she stepped outside, turning to give him a curious look from behind her mane of disheveled blond hair. Jessica's eyes flickered as they searched his for answers to questions she couldn't even begin to articulate.

In the morning light, with no makeup and her hair falling around her face like a yellow halo, he'd never seen any woman look more beautiful. His arms ached to pull her back into the condo, close the curtains, and lose himself in her beauty for the rest of the day, the rest of the week, the rest of his life.

"I want to come back tonight," she whispered.

"No," he said.

"Why not?"

"It's not safe."

"Does the school have people spying on professors or something? Who would even know whether I spent the night here or not?" she asked softly.

He saw the hurt and bewilderment in her face, and he balled his fists in frustration. It was horrible to tell a beautiful young woman with whom he was in love, and with whom he had just spent the night, that she had to leave and not come back. But he couldn't begin to explain the dangers that were attached to their relationship.

The light was beginning to illuminate the

dunes. "Come on," he said curtly. "I know it's hard to understand, but for now, you're just going to have to trust me." He took her arm and walked her firmly down the steps toward her red Jeep. He kissed her on the cheek and opened the door. "Drive carefully," he instructed. "And don't say anything to anyone. Promise me you won't say anything to anyone."

She settled herself into the driver's seat and pulled on her safety belt.

"Jessica!" he urged. "It's important. I know you don't think it's important—but it is. Promise me."

"I promise," she said softly. "When will I see you again?"

"I don't know. But I'll call you."

"To say good-bye?" she asked fearfully.

"No," he said vehemently. "To say I love you and I miss you and I want you and . . ."

She smiled, and he felt his lips curve unwillingly. This woman made him happy to be alive. And he hadn't felt that way in a long, long time. "And to tell you again that you can trust me," he finished.

That seemed to satisfy her, and she started the ignition. "I can really trust you?" she asked through the window as she put the Jeep in gear.

"You can really trust me," he assured her with an intimate smile.

He continued smiling as he watched the red Jeep disappear down the gray road that wound its way through the high, shrub-covered dunes.

Louis squinted into the distance, searching the

landscape for signs of movement. Sometimes he wondered if he were going mad. Becoming an obsessive-paranoid himself.

A cold sweat bathed his face. He suddenly realized it was very possible that he was being watched from some distant vantage point in the dunes.

The old house across the street was dark, as were the few houses that dotted the landscape. But he realized that there were gaps between the buildings that afforded a clear view of his condo from as far away as three miles.

A red Jeep would be easily spotted against the white sand from an even further distance.

He was mad, he decided. He'd been insane to let Jessica stay here. How could he have been so swept away by passion and affection that he let himself forget how dangerous any sign of an attachment could become?

What have I done? he wondered miserably.

Lila squeezed the toothpaste tube and immediately felt irritated. The center of the tube had been mashed almost flat. Furthermore, the mashing had caused a little tear to form on the side. Now green-and-red-striped toothpaste was shooting out at an angle all over her hand. Why couldn't he fold it neatly from the bottom like she did? "Bruce!" she said impatiently. "Bruce! Can you hear me?"

When there was no answer, Lila hoped it was because he was making coffee. She put the toothbrush in her mouth and vigorously attacked her upper teeth while her fingers searched the shelves for the bottle of specially formulated exfoliant she'd ordered from Paris. It was right behind Bruce's aftershave and her little basket of eye makeup. When she reached for it, the basket came tumbling down. Eight eye shadows, two lip liners, and a foundation sponge fell into the toilet, making a series of soft splashes. "Ommmphhh . . . noophhhh!" she cried.

"Did you say something?" she heard him call out from the other side of the bathroom door.

Lila jerked open the door. "Mmpphhs . . . ph-sooo . . . suphhh . . . phooo!"

He smiled. "Good morning to you, too."

She yanked the toothbrush from her mouth. "I said, why didn't you put the seat and the lid down on the toilet? I just knocked a whole bunch of stuff into it."

His face furrowed in concern. "Anything of mine?" he asked quickly.

Lila's foamy mouth fell open. "No! All my stuff. Eye shadows and lip liners."

He shrugged. "No big deal, then. You've got tons of makeup." He scratched his stubbly chin and yawned as if he had no further interest in the subject. "How much longer are you going to be?"

Lila gaped at him. Because of his carelessness, something important to her comfort and well-being was ruined. "You're so selfish."

"I am not selfish," he insisted. "I'm trying to get ready for school. This is not an earthshaking tragedy, and I want to know how much longer you're going to be in the bathroom."

"I'll be in touch," she said coldly, slamming the door.

He knocked angrily. "You know, Lila, part of the reason we're living together is so we can learn how to get along. It's supposed to be a lesson in give-and-take."

"Lesson one," she shouted. "Don't squeeze the toothpaste in the middle. Lesson two, don't leave the toilet seat up. Lesson three, don't act like your stuff is important and mine's not."

"Would you cut it out," he begged. "This is textbook. If you're going to be this picky, maybe I should go back and live at the frat house."

"Maybe you should," she responded angrily.

"You want to break up over some eye makeup?" he asked in a voice of disbelief.

"Hey! I got that misty gray in Paris. It's my favorite shade. It's the only one I've got. Now it's floating around in the potty and you don't even care."

"Lila!" Bruce yelled, sounding really angry now. "This isn't funny anymore. My first class is in twenty minutes. The professor locks the door when the bell rings. If you're late, you're out."

"So go take a shower at the frat house," she yelled, turning on the tap so hard that the noise from the gushing water drowned out his outraged shout and the thumping complaints of the tenant down below.

Chapter
Nineteen

_____

Winston pinched himself and then looked again at his reflection in the mirror. He didn't know whether to start laughing hysterically or burst into tears. "Trick or treat," he said to himself.

He turned sideways and then faced forward again. There really was something about a man in uniform—he looked ridiculous!

Winston sat down at his desk and let his head drop into his hands. He would never cheat again. Never. He'd learned his lesson, and the punishment was almost more than he could stand.

He'd never been as embarrassed in his whole life as he had been yesterday. His father had marched him over to the Reserve Officers' Training Corps office and signed him up as if he were sending Winston to summer camp.

They'd filled out several forms, which Winston had signed with a shaking hand. The next thing he knew, he was being handed pants, a jacket, boots, a hat, and a bewildering array of pins and doodads. He hadn't been able to figure out where those things were supposed to go, so he had thrust them down into his pocket like loose change.

He was due to report to his unit on the ROTC drill field located on the south side of campus in ten minutes. Maybe somebody there could show him what to do with the remaining gear. He stuffed the tie into his pocket and paused by the telephone. Should he call Denise again?

He'd left five messages on her machine yesterday and last night informing her that he was still a student, still in love, and now a soldier. But she hadn't called back.

No, he thought. *I can't call her again.* Obviously she despised him. And why shouldn't she? He was a cheater and a whiner.

Winston stepped out of his room and into the hall and was greeted by shrieks of surprise and gales of laughter from the girls who lived on his floor.

Through a complicated series of misspelled words and misread forms, Winston had wound up as the only male resident in an all-female dorm. Most of the time it was a lot of fun. But sometimes—times like this, for instance—it was hellacious. After spending most of the year surrounded by women, he'd decided that the fairer sex had a flair for ridicule that was deadlier than the most macho martial art.

"Winnie! What's the occasion?"

"Are you in a play or something?"

He smiled. "I joined ROTC," he said, trying hard to carry it off with nonchalance.

Maia, his resident adviser, came down the hall carrying a ten-pound weight and curling it with casual ease. She circled Winston with one eyebrow raised in skepticism. "I give him six weeks."

"No way," Anoushka argued. "Six days."

"A month," somebody else said.

"We'll have a floor pool. Everybody puts in a dollar. Winner take all."

"Ha ha," Winston said dryly. His ears felt bright red beneath the military cap. Nobody had said anything to him about the cheating. Maybe Denise had felt enough affection for him to keep from telling everyone what a low-down, rotten jerk he really was.

"Where were you last night?" Elizabeth snapped when Jessica walked in. She stood at her desk, shuffling impatiently through papers. Her exhausted face looked harried, angry, and relieved all at the same time. "I called Isabella. She said you were so upset you ran out of Theta house last night. So I thought maybe you went to Steven's. But nobody answered at his place." Her voice rose with mounting anger. "I've been frantic!" Elizabeth glanced at the clock. "Finally I called Todd and we agreed to wait fifteen more minutes before we called the police."

Jessica's mouth fell open. She had driven back

from Louis's condo in a fog of happiness, confusion, doubt, elation, anxiety, and all the other five thousand emotions that went along with falling madly in love. She'd been too preoccupied to concoct an alibi.

"Jess, what's going on? One minute you're lying in bed, saying you won't get up. The next minute you're gone all night. There's some very weird stuff going on in my life right now, and this is not a good time to disappear without warning."

"I'm sorry," Jessica said. "I was upset, and I didn't feel like sleeping or talking so I just . . . drove all night."

Elizabeth's brows rose in disbelief. "You drove all night?" She looked Jessica up and down and seemed to suddenly notice Jessica's ruined sweater with the bloodstain and her scraped forehead. Her face immediately registered alarm. "If you drove all night, what happened to your clothes and your face?" Her hand gripped Jessica's shoulder. "Jessica, tell me the truth. Did anybody do anything to you? Did somebody threaten you or try to rough you up?"

Jessica turned away and began peeling off her clothes, which were still damp from the storm last night. *Promise me you won't say anything to anyone.*

Jessica didn't like lying to Elizabeth. But she was in love. It was the kind of love that made people do terrible things. Jessica would steal for Louis. She would die for Louis. She would tell a thousand lies before she would break her word to him.

204

She rolled her eyes at Elizabeth's concern and laughed. "Come on. Of course nothing happened to me. I had an argument with Alison Quinn and left in a huff. It was raining when I ran out and I slipped and scraped my face on the pavement. It's not that big a deal. I had a lot on my mind. I didn't feel sleepy. So I drove the highways all night," she said in a subdued voice.

"Are you telling me the new guy didn't work out?"

"Um . . . yeah," Jessica lied. "I guess I was so disappointed, I wasn't thinking very clearly."

"I'm sorry, Jess. I hope you'll meet somebody soon. But please, don't ever do this to me again. You have no idea how worried I was."

Jessica lifted her head and smiled at Elizabeth.

When Elizabeth didn't smile back, Jessica felt a flicker of worry. Had she noticed the pink flush on Jessica's face? Did she realize Jessica was being less than truthful?

"I don't want to scare you," Elizabeth said. "But I want you to keep your eyes open."

Jessica frowned. "What do you mean?"

Elizabeth bit her lip and turned away. "I'm working on a story."

"A story about what?"

"About the athletics department."

"Again?"

Elizabeth looked slightly taken aback. "What do you mean, again?"

Jessica couldn't help laughing. "It seems like

you're always seeing some kind of conspiracy in the athletics department." Jessica pushed back her hair and smiled at Elizabeth. She didn't want to get into any arguments with her right now. Jessica was tired, and Elizabeth looked worn out and emotional.

Jessica decided the best thing to do was play along. "Do you think some of the jocks might bother me because of it?"

"It's possible."

"I'll keep my eyes open," Jessica agreed. "But they'd better look out for me." She reached into her closet for some clean clothes. Even if Elizabeth wasn't being paranoid, who cared about some stupid jocks? Nothing connected with the school or the athletics department or her sorority or anything else seemed important anymore. "Do you need the Jeep?"

"No. Why?"

"Because I want to run into town," Jessica answered. She'd seen a book in the window of the Main Street Bookstall. A book on medieval tapestries. She'd noticed the cover because it had featured a blond woman, who looked very much like herself, with a unicorn.

Last night she and Louis had lain awake, talking for hours before she'd fallen asleep with her head on his chest. Louis had laughed a lot when she'd told him about her childhood. Jessica had been a proud member of the Unicorns, a club made up of all the prettiest and most popular girls at Sweet Valley Middle School.

Yawning, Louis had commented that he liked the image of her with a unicorn. Then he closed his eyes, saying it was the picture he wanted to carry with him into his dreams.

Jessica wanted to give him the book and tell him to keep it in his condo. It would be a symbol that she wanted to be a permanent part of his life.

Elizabeth picked up her backpack, pulled her baseball cap down over her blond hair, and hesitated at the door. "Fine with me. I don't need the Jeep. But Jessica," she said. "Be careful, okay?"

Jessica rolled her eyes.

Winston crossed the street that separated the south side of the campus from the ROTC drill field, carrying his ROTC papers under his arm. He'd never been so unhappy, scared, and humiliated in his entire life. *I can't believe this is happening to me,* he thought. He'd gone from Winston Egbert, class clown, to Winston Egbert, cheater. It was worse than being branded a coward.

And the punishment was worse, too. Morning marches. Drills. Uniforms. Exercises. Shouting. All the things he hated doing.

Several yards away, he could see the SVU ROTC unit falling into formation on the field. A lone figure detached itself from the marching column and walked briskly in his direction.

If only I could talk to Denise, he mourned. *If only we could laugh about this together, it wouldn't seem as awful as it truly is.*

But Denise had shut him out of her life completely. He didn't blame her. What he had done was despicable and inexcusable. The only thing he could hope for was that he could parlay his ROTC experience into an army commission. Maybe even become a member of one of those elite special forces that spent their time diffusing car bombs and learning nine ways to kill terrorists using handy household implements.

He let his imagination run loose, picturing himself twenty pounds heavier—with enormous shoulders and arms.

A political catastrophe in some far-flung corner of the world might threaten the safety and security of the forces of democracy. The commander would assemble his elite forces and ask for volunteers—intrepid warriors willing to embark on what could only be described as a suicide mission.

After a short but dramatic pause, the brooding and emotionally mysterious Winston Egbert would step bravely forward. "I'll go," he'd say in a deep baritone.

His commander would put a hand on his shoulder. His eyes would fill with tears. "Anything you want me to tell your folks?"

"No, sir," Winston would say, reaching for his gun and strapping on his parachute. "Just tell Denise Waters that I love her. And that I'm sorry."

He had a picture of himself, noble and uncomplaining, walking off into the morning mist. Winston was so moved by his own sacrifice that his eyes filled with tears, and the figure moving toward him dissolved into a salty blur.

"Winston!" The voice snapped him out of his daydream.

As the person came closer, he realized that it was a girl.

"Winston!" the voice said again. "Aren't you going to say anything?"

Winston rubbed his eyes with his knuckles. When the blur cleared, his eyeballs nearly bulged out of their sockets. The little soldier was none other than Denise, dressed in full ROTC regalia.

His mouth opened and closed, but he was so astonished, he couldn't speak. She shifted her rifle from one shoulder to the other. "I thought about it a long time, Winston," she said. "What you did was wrong. But I love you anyway. Where you go, I go. If you go in the army, I go in the army."

"I thought I'd lost you," he whispered hoarsely. "I thought I'd finally done something so awful that you'd never want to see me again."

She set down the gun and put her arms around him. "Oh, Winston," she said. "Sometimes you're so goofy."

A shrill whistle startled them, and they broke apart. A large officer bore down upon them. "No fraternizing during drill," he yelled at Denise. "Who are you?" he demanded of Winston.

Denise straightened up, saluted with a white glove, and took Winston's papers from his hand. "Sir. This is Winston Egbert, sir. He's our new recruit, sir!"

The large guy looked Winston up and down. Winston stood up as straight as he possibly could and threw out his chest.

"New recruit, eh?" he said.

"Yep!" Winston said cheerfully.

"That's yes, sir, to you," the officer shouted in his face.

"Soreeeee," Winston responded automatically.

"What?"

"I mean, I'm sorry, sir." He cut his eyes toward Denise, expecting her to giggle helplessly at this guy's antics.

Oddly enough, Denise didn't look amused. She was actually watching this GI Joe wanna-be with admiring eyes.

"You may rejoin the regiment, Private Waters."

"Sir. Yes, sir." Denise executed a crisp salute, clicked her heels while doing a smooth one hundred and eighty degree turn, and walked briskly back toward the marching line of young men and women.

Some second-in-command type was leading the squad, yelling out variations of, "One, two, three, four. One, two, three, four." It was kind of mesmerizing when Winston started getting into it.

"I've heard about you, Egbert," the officer said. His tone indicated that what he had heard was quite unfavorable.

Winston didn't know what to say to that. A mild, "Oh, really?" was the best he could manage.

"We're going to make a man out of you," the officer asserted.

"My father will be very glad to hear that, sir." Winston gulped.

The officer's eyes followed Denise's trim figure as she marched smartly with the others. "She's a fine recruit, Egbert."

"Yes, sir."

"She's only been on board a few hours and already she's a credit to the unit." He turned his forbidding gaze in Winston's direction. "See that you are, too."

"Yes, sir," Winston said, pulling himself up. Denise had the right attitude, he decided. This guy might look like a toy soldier, but he'd probably fall on his sword before he'd do something like cheat on a test.

There was a lot to be learned here. And Winston was determined to apply himself. He had a lot of work ahead of him—winning back the respect of his father, his mother, Professor Stark, his friends, and most important of all—Denise.

"So Jessica finally showed up?"

Elizabeth nodded and related the events of that morning to Todd.

Todd took a bite of his sandwich. "Where was she? Or is it none of my business?"

Elizabeth poked her chicken salad with disinterest. As usual, the cafeteria was packed at lunchtime. Bright sunlight streamed through the windows, and they were surrounded by laughing, chattering people. Behind the shining chrome

211

counters work-study students in bright yellow uniforms smiled and joked with each other as they made sandwiches and ladled soup into bowls.

Everything seemed so normal and innocent, it was hard to believe that something sinister and dark was happening all around them. "She said she was driving all night."

"Think that's true?"

"I don't know," Elizabeth said uneasily. "But I don't like the idea of Jessica running around with all this weird stuff going on."

"Maybe it's time for you to bow out of this thing."

"We've had this conversation before," Elizabeth said. "I didn't bow out then and I'm not bowing out now. It's my investigation."

"And it's my career."

"So?"

"So my career isn't worth risking your safety or Jessica's. For that matter, it's not worth mine."

Elizabeth lifted her eyebrows. "That's not what you told Santos."

Todd flushed. "Yeah, well . . . What can I say? I had a macho attack."

"Yeah, well . . . I'm having one too. I'm not letting anyone bully me into backing down and that's all there is to it."

Todd held up his hands. "That's been easy since Santos hasn't made any attempt to bully you or Jessica."

Elizabeth's feet fidgeted nervously under the

212

table. "You know, I don't think Santos will do anything unless he's provoked."

"But that doesn't mean he's not dangerous. So far, he's just been letting us wear ourselves out running around in circles. At some point, though, he's going to fight back. We need to keep our eyes open . . . be prepared."

Elizabeth yawned, stretched her arms over her head, and laughed. "So much for keeping my eyes open. Listen, I didn't get any sleep last night, so I'm going back to my room to take a nap before my next class."

"I'm going to the gym," Todd said, hoisting on his backpack and standing up. "I haven't had a workout in days and who knows, maybe I'll find out something new."

Elizabeth watched Todd exit the cafeteria and hoisted her own backpack with a sinking feeling in her stomach. She couldn't stop thinking that she and Todd were walking toward an invisible ledge. The lip was someplace near, almost in reach, but they wouldn't know they'd found it until it was too late and they'd stepped over the edge.

Chapter
Twenty

Jessica carefully arranged the beautifully wrapped book on the seat beside her. The paper was green-and-black check, with a green-and-black-striped ribbon tied around it.

She started the Jeep, glanced in the rearview mirror, and saw a black Mazda idling in the street several car lengths behind her.

Strange. That black Mazda's been behind me the entire way into town from campus.

Jessica threw the Jeep in gear and pulled out into the street. The Mazda pulled out too. *Hmmmm?* Maybe Elizabeth wasn't being completely paranoid. Maybe some jock thought Jessica was Elizabeth and was trying to intimidate her by following her around town.

Jessica let out a snort of contempt. It would take more than a jock in a black Mazda to ruin her day. She rolled her head around on her shoulders, loosening the muscles and remembering the warm comfort of Louis's hands on the back of her neck. His fingers had combed through her hair and followed the strands down to the middle of her back. The memory raised a trail of goose bumps along her spine.

"What . . ." Jessica screamed when a sudden, hard bump interrupted her daydream. Her hands tightened on the wheel of the Jeep to keep it from lurching into the wrong lane.

Glaring into the rearview mirror, Jessica hoped to catch a glimpse of the driver's face. The black Mazda dropped back. Jessica pressed the gas pedal and sped toward the entrance ramp of the highway that led back to campus. *It's time to lose this goon, whoever he is.*

The needle on the speedometer climbed steadily and leveled off when she merged into the traffic. Behind her, the Mazda wove aggressively through the traffic, trying to catch up.

Jessica wasn't too worried. If this jock wanted to play bumper cars, her red Jeep was better equipped to take a few blows to the fender than the fancy Mazda.

The Mazda dropped back again, and Jessica let out her breath. She had a feeling he'd made his point. *I hope this is Liz's last investigation of the athletics department,* Jessica thought wryly.

For the next five miles, the Mazda followed at a distance. The traffic was approaching a section of road that was under construction. A black-and-yellow sign read SLOW and signaled that the road curved sharply.

Jessica watched the Mazda as it zoomed up and scooted around the car behind her so that it could follow her more closely. Her pulse quickened, and she pressed the gas pedal reluctantly. She knew she should slow down, but he was bearing down on her. If he didn't slow down, he was going to . . .

"Oh, no!" Jessica yelled out loud when she realized he had no intention of stopping.

The guy was some kind of maniac. If he didn't slow down, he'd rear-end her. He was going to kill them both.

Jessica slammed her foot on the gas, accelerating forward with the jock on her tail. Faster and faster went the Jeep as the road led higher and higher up the twisting, turning mountain highway.

Louis made himself a cup of tea, took a sip, and walked back over to his desk, determined to get his mind off Jessica and his fears for her. He had a pile of papers he needed to grade—by late this afternoon, if possible.

He'd been trying all morning to forget her beautiful face, her soothing voice, long enough to get some work done. But it had been impossible. The room was too full of memories. He was hopelessly in love.

The logs in the fireplace snapped and popped. It was actually too balmy a day for a fire, and he was uncomfortably warm. But the friendly flicker made the room feel less lonely without her. He thought about going for a cold swim until a glance at his watch reminded him that he had a class in an hour. It would take too long to swim, shower, and get dressed again.

The phone rang and he reached for it, half hoping, half fearing it was Jessica. "Hello," Louis said breathlessly.

There was no answer.

"Hello?" he repeated.

Through the phone, he heard the distant sound of tires screeching and a horn honking.

"Hello?" he said again.

"Who is she?" a familiar voice demanded.

A fist clutched at Louis's heart and squeezed. "Leave her alone," he said evenly.

There was a laugh on the other end of the line. A laugh punctuated with static.

"Where are you?" he asked.

"I'm in a car," she said calmly. "Going about eighty miles an hour. Guess who's in front of me? About five inches in front of me."

Louis heard another squeal of tires, and he felt the fear in his heart radiate through his body. "What are you doing?" he whispered.

"I'm getting ready to run Blondie off I-87 at the Pine Bluff construction site," she replied calmly. "I'm going to kill her, Louis. And I just thought you might like to listen while I do it. I warned you a long time ago that I wasn't going to stand by and watch you fall in love with someone else."

"Leave her alone, Chloe," he bellowed. "Leave her alone!"

Her only answer was the insane laugh he had come to fear and hate. He heard a horn. He heard a bang. He heard another screech of rubber against the concrete.

Louis gripped the phone so tightly he felt the bones of his knuckles practically pop through his skin. "Leave her alone!" he yelled in helpless, impotent fury.

He could see Jessica, driving for her life along the stretch of road that was treacherous under the best of circumstances. The construction made it an obstacle course. With a driver determined to run her off the road, Jessica might panic.

He pictured the red Jeep crashing through the flimsy barrier, falling through the air, and crashing onto the rocks below with Jessica's fragile body inside it.

"She's no threat to you," Louis said. "Why are you doing this?" But even as he said it, he knew it was no use. Logic. Reason. Rational emotion. None of it made any difference. And none of it would save Jessica from the fate he had dreaded for her from the moment of their first conversation on the beach. There was a horrific, metallic crashing sound. "Jessica!" he screamed.

Chapter Twenty-one

Mark placed a stack of fresh towels in the towel bin and removed the web of keys that hung from his belt. He let himself and Coach Crane into the equipment cage and marveled at Mr. Santos's clout. Last night, Mark Gathers was nobody. This morning, he was Coach Crane's student assistant and best buddy. "After you get through taking inventory, go hang around the basketball court and watch the guys practice." Coach Crane winked. "We've got some new guys you don't know. And you ought to get to know 'em. I have a feeling they're going to be your teammates pretty soon."

"Thanks, Coach."

"Call me if you need anything." Coach Crane gave Mark a friendly smack on the arm with the inventory sheet and pressed it into his hand. "Don't forget to lock up before you leave." He straightened the bill of his SVU athletics cap and strode toward the exit. "I'll be in my office if anybody asks."

Mark had always been a bit afraid of Coach Crane. He was a tall, broad, athletic man in his sixties with a massive jaw and thick gray hair. His usual attire was a gray sweatshirt, gray sweatpants, white athletic shoes, and a shiny whistle around his neck.

He rarely smiled and he was a strict disciplinarian—with his staff as well as his students. Coach Crane was the head coach. That meant he oversaw the entire athletics program. Under him were a variety of team coaches, all of whom reported directly to Coach Crane. Crane was the ultimate authority and what he said, went.

Mark quickly counted the basketballs and jerseys, ticked them off on the list, and closed the cage. He left the equipment room and walked toward the gym with a slight ache around his heart. This had been his turf once. His and Todd's. They'd been the stars of the SVU basketball team until Elizabeth Wakefield's investigation had disgraced them.

"Gathers!" Mark turned and smiled as Ben Alsup and another former teammate came striding down the hallway. "Glad you decided to stick around," he said happily, shaking Mark's arm. "Coach Crane said you were working here. What's the story, man?"

Before Mark could answer, the front doors opened and a group of girls came walking in, headed for the weight room. He froze. One of them was Alex.

She saw him and did a double take. "Mark!" she exclaimed, coming to a stop. "What are you doing here?"

Mark wished he could just evaporate into thin air. Alex was the last person he wanted to deal with right now. He shrugged. "This and that," he replied vaguely.

"How have you been?" she asked shyly.

"Fine," he said, infusing a defensive warning note into his voice. Alex had a bad habit of asking a lot of questions . . . too many questions. He wanted to discourage her from launching into a big interrogation right here with a bunch of people around.

He saw a red sheen of anger creep across her translucent skin. He remembered that pink flush from the old days. It actually made her look even prettier. The color made her hazel eyes turn bottle green and brought out the highlights in her coppery hair, which was piled high on her head today.

Alex's long legs and torso were encased in a yellow unitard, worn with baggy shorts. She looked like she'd been working out. Her arms and calves had a shapely definition. Strong, but feminine.

"You look good," Mark said, trying to keep the defensive note out of his voice and make the exchange pleasant.

Her tense face relaxed, but she didn't look gratified.

"Any chance you might be back on the team?" one of the guys asked before Alex could say anything.

221

"Absolutely," Mark replied. "I had a talk with Dr. Beal and Coach Crane this morning. I think we can safely say I'll be back on the team by next semester."

There was a gasp, and everybody turned toward the door. Todd Wilkins stood there, staring at Mark. "You're getting back on the team?" he asked quietly.

Mark met his stare and didn't look away. "That's right. Courtesy of Dr. Beal, Coach Crane, and our mutual friend, T. Clay."

"Mark!" Everybody snapped to attention when Coach Crane appeared.

"Yes, sir?"

Coach Crane gave Todd an unfriendly look and signaled to Mark that he wanted to speak with him privately.

"I'll see you around," Mark said to Alex. He turned away from her and hurried to Coach Crane's side. "Coach?"

Coach Crane licked the envelope in his hand and gave it to Mark. "Take this to Dr. Beal. And wait for an answer."

Elizabeth heard the phone as she turned the key in the lock and opened the door of her dorm room. She dropped her backpack on the floor, smothering a yawn as she picked up the phone. "Hello?"

"Ms. Elizabeth Wakefield, please."

"Speaking," Elizabeth answered.

"This is Dr. Beal's secretary," a woman said in a clipped, efficient voice. "Dr. Beal would like to meet with you in his office."

Elizabeth's brows lifted in surprise. "All right," she agreed. "When?"

"Would right now be convenient?"

Elizabeth looked at her watch. "Yes. Okay. I'll walk on over."

"Very good, Ms. Wakefield. Dr. Beal will be expecting you." Even the way she hung up the phone seemed clipped and efficient.

Elizabeth wondered if she should call Todd and tell him. No. He was on his way to the gym for a workout. She'd probably be back in her room before he returned.

She quickly left the dorm room, hurried down the stairs, and exited through the side door of Dickenson. If she cut diagonally across the campus, the administration building was only a few minutes away.

Elizabeth quickened her step. She couldn't wait to know what Dr. Beal could possibly have to tell her.

When she reached the administration building, Elizabeth couldn't help noticing how the athletics complex loomed over it from behind.

It had never occurred to her until now just how symbolic that was.

Her mind raced ahead, exploring the possibility of using that image as the lead-in to the story she hoped to crack very soon. She was still mentally composing copy for the voice-over by the time she reached Dr. Beal's office on the second floor. Elizabeth opened the heavy wooden door. A secretary sat in an outer office behind a desk piled high with paperwork. "Ms. Wakefield?"

"That's me."

"He's waiting." She nodded toward another wooden door that led to an inner office. "Go right in."

Elizabeth complied, letting herself into Dr. Beal's office. He sat behind a long, black marble-topped desk with a sheaf of papers in his hand. "Sit down," he said without looking up.

The shade had been pulled down over the single large window that looked out over the campus quadrangle. The walls of the office were paneled with dark wood. Light from the green desk lamp cast a glare across the black marble. It was like being in a climate-controlled cave, Elizabeth decided.

She sat down on the edge of her chair, tense.

Dr. Beal lifted his eyes and looked at Elizabeth. There was so much animosity in the glance, she involuntarily flinched. "I understand you and Mr. Wilkins visited Mr. Santos."

"That's right."

"According to Mr. Santos, you were both quite accusatory. I must remind you that Mr. Santos is the head of the Alumni Association and a principal donor to this university. Without his help and support many fine programs, including the new science lab, the language arts center, and the campus station, WSVU, would not be possible. I must ask, I must insist, rather, that you cease your attempt to discredit him. It is rude, insulting, and disrespectful."

Elizabeth swallowed. "And what if I don't?" she asked in a neutral voice.

Dr. Beal smiled. "It would be very unfortunate to have to expel your sister, Ms. Wakefield. But if necessary, it can be done."

"Expel Jessica!" Elizabeth cried. "Expel her for what?"

"For helping Winston Egbert to cheat," he said calmly.

"What!"

Dr. Beal picked up a piece of paper, read it again as if refreshing himself with the contents, and smiled. "According to the statement made by Mr. Winston Egbert, he was able to procure a copy of Professor Stark's physics test with the help of Jessica Wakefield."

"That's a lie," Elizabeth said, standing up. "I don't know what you're talking about. But I know my sister, and she's never helped anybody to cheat."

"Sit down, Ms. Wakefield. And please lower your voice."

"I'll fight back. She'll fight back. We'll fight back," she insisted.

"I don't think you will."

"Why not?"

"Because then you would force me to have these made public." He threw something down on the desk for Elizabeth to see in the harsh glare of the desk lamp. Her mouth fell open. "Oh!" she gasped.

"Shocking, aren't they?" he commented pleasantly.

With a shaking hand, Elizabeth reached down and gingerly picked up one of the photos. It was a picture of Jessica locked in a passionate embrace with Professor Miles, the new campus heartthrob. It looked as if it had been taken at a beach house. Jessica's hair was a mess, and the shoulder of her white sweater had slipped down. The pictures told a fairly convincing story of what had gone on at the beach house last night.

I was driving all night, Jessica had said.

Elizabeth was torn between outrage over the invasion of her sister's privacy and anger over her sister's duplicity.

"I'm sure you know the school's policy regarding sexual relationships between students and professors. It would be a shame for us to have to fire Professor Miles and subject your sister to a lot of embarrassing publicity, but . . ."

"This is blackmail," Elizabeth interrupted, tears of rage streaming down her cheeks. She shoved the pictures across the table.

Dr. Beal pushed them back in her direction. "Those are yours to keep. I have other copies . . . many other copies." He stood up. "Ms. Wakefield, this meeting is over. And so is your investigation. In the interests of everyone involved, I strongly suggest that you terminate any and all interviews you may have arranged with former players and SVU personnel. It would be a fruitless search for scandal, and frankly, this school has had enough damage to its reputation . . . thanks to you."

He walked over to the door and opened it. "Ms. Willis," he said, his voice changing in an instant from threatening to cordial. "Would you see Ms. Wakefield out, please."

Ms. Willis brushed past Mark and haughtily opened the door to the hallway, inviting Elizabeth to leave.

Elizabeth stood in the doorway next to Dr. Beal, her eyes flashing. Mark had never seen any girl look as angry as Elizabeth Wakefield did right now.

As soon as she saw him, Elizabeth's eyes blazed. "You!" she said in a voice of deep loathing. "Why did you come back here?"

Mark smiled. "Because you asked me to. You and Wilkins."

Elizabeth's lip lifted in a sneer. "Our mistake. We should have left you under the rock you crawled out from."

Dr. Beal's secretary let out a shocked gasp, and Dr. Beal stepped forward. "Ms. Wakefield," he barked. "I will not tolerate rudeness to anyone in this office, particularly an employee of the school."

"Employee of the school!" Elizabeth exclaimed.

Mark couldn't help smiling. "Student assistant to the athletics department."

"But he's not a student," Elizabeth argued.

"Mr. Gathers is on academic hold right now," Dr. Beal said calmly. "It's difficult to re-enroll a student at mid-semester."

"Then he's still not a student," Elizabeth argued loudly. "And he doesn't have any business on the athletics department's payroll."

Mark grabbed her arm and pushed her out the door. "Let me go!" she yelled.

Dr. Beal and his secretary jumped forward. Dr. Beal grabbed Mark's arms, and his secretary took Elizabeth's arm. "Ms. Wakefield! Mr. Gathers!" she said sharply. "Control yourselves, or I'll call the campus police."

Mark and Elizabeth broke apart.

"Let me remind you, Ms. Wakefield, that I can suspend any student I consider to be disruptive or potentially disruptive." Elizabeth yanked her arm out of Ms. Willis's grasp. The envelope in her hand fell to the ground, spilling the contents in a pile on the rug. It looked like pictures. Mark bent to pick them up. He felt his jaw drop. "Oh, my . . ."

She knocked them from his hands, and they flew in every direction. Gasping and beginning to sob, Elizabeth scurried around on the floor, collecting them.

"Come in, Mark," Dr. Beal said curtly.

Mark stepped into Dr. Beal's office. "Close the door," he instructed. Mark closed the door on Elizabeth and the surprised secretary and handed Dr. Beal the envelope from Coach Crane. Dr. Beal opened it and unfolded several large ledger sheets. Mark recognized the type of paper from his accounting class.

"Television goes to people's heads." Dr. Beal

sniffed and studied the green pages. "Year after year these student reporters make a nuisance of themselves."

"She sure shot down my career," Mark commented.

Dr. Beal smiled. "We'll have to see what we can do about that. Mr. Santos seems to think we should put you back on the team as soon as possible."

Mark smiled back. "I'd really like that."

Dr. Beal sat down at his personal computer, pulled up a program, and began to enter some data, referring to the sheets.

Mark strained his eyes to read the screen. CAPITAL BUILDING FUND was printed in large letters across the top.

"That about the construction being done on campus?"

Dr. Beal swiveled in his chair. "Yes. Why do you ask?"

Mark sensed immediately that he'd asked a wrong question. "Just curious." He laughed uneasily. "As the student assistant to the athletics department, I'm just trying to keep up with what's going on."

"Very commendable," Dr. Beal said. "But Mark . . . how shall I put this? Don't make the same mistake Ms. Wakefield and her friend, Mr. Wilkins, are making. Don't be too curious. And don't be overeager."

Jessica climbed out of the Jeep and held on to the door handle for support. Her legs were shaking so badly, she wasn't sure she could make it to the dorm from the parking lot.

She swallowed several times, fighting the queasy feeling in the back of her throat. She walked around the Jeep, inspecting the damage.

It's not half as bad as I thought. There was a huge dent in the right rear bumper. Two hubcaps had been knocked off, and the muffler had fallen out about two miles back. She'd dragged it onto the campus with sparks flying along the pavement.

Jessica's mind struggled hard to comprehend what had just happened. Somebody had tried to kill her. Really tried to kill her.

Running somebody off the bluff wasn't a prank. It was a serious murder attempt. And her escape had been a serious suicide attempt. Jessica had jumped a construction hurdle, cut across four lanes of oncoming traffic, executed a U-turn, and exited on an entrance ramp.

It was a good trick, but she hoped she never had to do it again. Nobody could survive it twice.

She needed to call the police and report what had happened. But she wanted to talk to Elizabeth first. Obviously this had something to do with her investigation.

Trembling with fear and post-traumatic stress, Jessica grabbed the gift for Louis and hugged it a moment for comfort. "I'm so glad I didn't die," she wept gratefully into the ribbon. "Not now that I've found Louis."

With a deft motion, she grabbed the insurance

information from the glove compartment, slapped it shut, and jumped from the Jeep.

"Excuse me. Excuse me, miss."

A woman walked toward Jessica from the opposite end of the parking lot. She was tall and dramatic with a full, shapely figure and long, curly black hair that hung around her shoulders. Her lips were a bright red, and she wore a black dress. "I'd like to talk to you," the woman began.

"This really isn't a good time," Jessica said breathlessly. Her mind was spinning so fast, it was hard to concentrate. And she couldn't imagine what this woman wanted to talk about. She was probably selling something or maybe she was a representative for some weird religious group. Either way, Jessica didn't want to get caught in some long conversation. "Maybe tomorrow." She turned and hurried toward the door of the dorm.

"I want to talk to you about my husband," the woman said.

A shrill alarm sounded in Jessica's brain. She dropped the gift and turned slowly.

The woman's face wore a look of malicious triumph. "That's right," she said. "My husband is Louis Miles. And I'm warning you to stay away from him."

Husband?

Louis was married.

Jessica moaned and doubled over as if she'd been hit in the stomach. No wonder he was so worried about being seen. No wonder he'd been so adamant about secrecy.

The woman stepped close. Too close. She wore a thick, sweet, cloying perfume that made Jessica's head hurt. "Stay away from my husband," she hissed. "If you don't, you'd better look for me in your rearview mirror every single minute of the rest of your life."

Now that Jessica has met the other woman, will she dump Louis or risk her life for the man she loves? Find out in Sweet Valley University 17, **DEADLY ATTRACTION.**

We hope you enjoyed reading this book. If you would like to receive further information about available titles in the Bantam series, just write to the address below, with your name and address:

KIM PRIOR
Bantam Books
61–63 Uxbridge Road
London W5 5SA

If you live in Australia or New Zealand and would like more information about the series, please write to:

SALLY PORTER
Transworld Publishers (Australia) Pty Ltd
15–25 Helles Avenue
Moorebank
NSW 2170
AUSTRALIA

KIRI MARTIN
Transworld Publishers (NZ) Ltd
3 William Pickering Drive
Albany
Auckland
NEW ZEALAND

All Transworld titles are available by post from:-
Bookservice by Post
PO Box 29
Douglas
Isle of Man
IM99 1BQ

Credit Cards accepted. Please telephone 01624 675137 or
fax 01624 670923

Please allow £0.75 per book for post and packing UK.
Overseas customers allow £1.00 per book for post and
packing.